Believe - In Love - Always

Stories of Love, Longing and Togetherness

Stars from the Borderless Sea

SHALINI MULLICK

Readomania

Readomania
An imprint of Kurious Kind Media Private Limited
readomania.com
email: contact@readomania.com
Facebook: facebook.com/iamreadomania
Twitter: twitter.com/iamreadomania
Instagram: iamreadomania

First Published in 2022 by Readomania

ISBN: 978-93-91800-22-2

Typeset in Palatino Linotype by Shine Graphics
Printed in Delhi

Out beyond the ideas of wrongdoing and rightdoing
there is a field. I'll meet you there.

—Rumi

Dedicated

to

Amrit Grover

The Stories

Sayonee

Sayonee – Soulmate

∞∞∞

Lovers don't finally meet somewhere. They're in each other all along.

—Rumi

∞∞∞

1

Geetika sat down at the kitchen counter with her cup of coffee. Next to her was the stack of newspapers her neighbour Rita had brought her last evening. Geetika looked forward to Rita's regular visits, not just because of the newspapers she brought but also for a chance to speak in Hindi. Rita worked as a flight attendant and would often bring back Indian newspapers from her trips to Delhi. Geetika hadn't taken to reading newspapers online yet. *Nothing like the rustle of newsprint*, she was wont to tell everyone and enjoy catching up on news from back home, even if it was slightly dated.

Last evening, Rita's usual anecdotes about the passengers on her flight had given way to a discussion about Geetika's forthcoming trip to India. It was a result of the excitement Gaurav had built up in his telephone calls; an excitement that had rubbed off the entire family. Gaurav, her younger son had finally fallen in love. And everyone was looking forward to the engagement, slated to take place in India in a few weeks.

The pressure cooker was whistling, releasing turmeric-tinged pungent steam. The sky outside was overcast. It was too early in the morning to guess if the sun would find its way through the clouds. On many days, sunshine remained elusive. But the California gloom didn't bother her. There were a good number of sunny days too, after all.

She reached for her reading glasses and picked up the newspaper on top of the pile.

The Times of India
Delhi Edition
8 June 2005

Indo-Nepal ties dominated the headlines, but her attention wandered to a tiny news piece somewhere below. It stood out from other news items.

Founder of India's premier military intelligence institute passes away

Suddenly, the black letters seemed out of focus, floating on the white background. She was oblivious to the insistent whistles of the pressure cooker. A few moments later, the fuzziness settled, and she read the next few lines.

Major (Retd.) Shekhar Kumar, passed away at his residence in Uttarakhand last night. He was the founder of the Indian Organisation of Military Intelligence (IOMI). A Param Vir Chakra awardee, he fought with distinction in the 1971 Indo-Pak war. His second innings with the Indian armed forces as a military intelligence expert was equally illustrious. He was instrumental in raising India's first secret service force.

Contd. on Page 3

Her mind was playing tricks on her. This could not be real. She turned to Page 3 and navigated through the columns to find what she was looking for.

Contd. from Page 1

As founder-director of IOMI, Major (Retd.) Shekhar Kumar charted the course of the prestigious organisation. With his characteristic vision and professional brilliance, he digitalised many defence operations, making India a pioneer in such initiatives. The support lent by IOMI to India's armed forces in the Kargil War and other counter-insurgency operations was invaluable. Kumar was awarded the Padma Bhushan for his service to the country. A believer in his simple roots and humble beginnings, he had recently retired to his native village in Uttarakhand. He is survived by his wife and daughter.

The photo from the Param Vir Chakra Award ceremony showed him in uniform, complete with the coveted bronze medal. The glint in his eyes shone through the haziness of the picture. There was a picture from the Padma Bhushan ceremony too, and another from a defence ministry briefing.

Shekhar had been a regular at the official briefings during the extensive TV coverage of the Kargil War. Seeing him on TV, at almost touching distance, had seemed surreal to Geetika. *Major Shekhar Kumar (Retd.), Defence Strategist*, the captions had read. Complete yet inadequate, as captions often are. She would tune into the reportage, but the rhetoric and call for war from armchair warriors would make her uncomfortable. What did these youth know about war? How could anyone ask for combat sitting in their plush homes, oblivious to the reality of a soldier's life? They would never know the pain and anguish war brought upon so many of their countrymen; how their families waited for news, never completely ready to hear what they had always prepared themselves for.

Her mind fixated itself on its tirade on the futility of war. But her heart knew that she needed to return to the news item.

2

"Mom, everything fine? You seem lost. And the cooker is puffing away!"

She had not noticed Gopal come into the kitchen.

"Uh! Hmm. Nothing, dear. I forgot all about the dal. Please turn it off."

"Of course…the newspaper," Gopal said and smiled.

It was both a relief and a surprise that her turmoil was not evident to him.

"I'll book the tickets for the India trip today. The girls are so excited and have been pestering Gaurav to send us a photo of his fiancée for days," he said with a chuckle.

She watched silently as he rushed through his breakfast.

He hugged her before leaving for work.

"Make sure you get some fresh air, Ma. You are looking tired. See you in the evening!"

Geetika had adjusted well to life in Gopal and Veena's new home. She found the rhythm and routine of daily life comforting. The picturesque and serene patio was her favourite spot, where she would spend her mornings reading or knitting. The last few days, however, she had been busy making lists. Shopping lists for Gaurav's engagement; gifts for his fiancée and things to pack for their trip to India.

In the tranquillity of this Californian suburb, she often found herself thinking about the simple life of her growing-up years. She would find parallels between life here and the life of her childhood. The archways and spiral staircases of this sprawling Spanish-style bungalow were like those of her childhood home. The expanse of greenery reminded her of the large, manicured gardens of their royal estate. The tall deodar trees, fountains, marble statues and ornate decorations of the estate, and the private balconies, spacious rooms, and large corridors of the palace would come alive in her mind. But a split instant later, it would seem as if it had all been in another lifetime. And, in so many ways, it had.

She made her way to the swing on the patio and continued to read the news report.

Senior politicians and defence officials have expressed their grief. A state funeral and a 21-gun salute have been announced in his honour.

She felt a crushing pain constricting her chest. It rose, like a tidal wave that would drown her. And then, she felt nothing. Maybe her heart had stopped. She sat there completely still, feet planted on the floor, not allowing even the slightest movement of the swing. After what seemed like ages, she heard a voice insist that she make the tempering for the dal. She realised that it was coming from her head. Her brain was trying to take charge of the situation. On the other hand, her heart silenced by the waves of pain, timidly whispered, "Just a little while longer." It wasn't like she needed to eat the dal right now, after all. She was a detached spectator in this battle between heart and head.

The sky was grey and foggy. She could feel the sultriness of air saturated with moisture. Tears, she realised. The constriction relaxed and was replaced by the tears that formed a lump somewhere in her throat.

More than an hour later, the skies remained overcast and the newspaper, in her hands. The lump in her throat had become bigger and heavier. Maybe she could leave it behind, here, on the patio, with the newspaper? If she got on with her routine, perhaps the day would unfold exactly as it would have if Rita hadn't popped in with her vivacious smile and the newspapers?

I must go indoors, she decided.

She imagined Gopal's voice telling her not to get up suddenly; the stern but loving reminder that parents find strange coming from their children. Today though, she was grateful for the advice and waited a few moments after standing up. Finally, sure that her legs wouldn't give way, she went inside.

Mechanically, she headed towards the kitchen. *Must finish my chores,* her brain insisted.

The crackle of the cumin seeds filled the kitchen as she diced the tomatoes. Carefully separating the coriander leaves from the stems, she chopped and washed them. Fat separated from the tomatoes, and the colour of the dal changed to a perfect orange. She topped the bowl of lentils with the coriander and neatly slit green chilies.

Just then, suddenly, the fog of disbelief clouded her thoughts again. She felt herself going numb. Standing there by the kitchen counter, she was seized by an irrational loathing for what she was cooking. In a split second, she lifted the container of dal and tipped the aromatic preparation into the garbage bin. She then made her way to her room.

Geetika's airy and well-lit room opened into her tiny kitchen garden in the backyard. Many of her plants had taken root in the last few months. On weekends, her granddaughters joined her in tending the green patch. Tara and Uma filled the house with laughter, and Geetika's life with happiness. Geetika would fuss over the girls. They loved the fragrant dollop of ghee she would add to their mashed potatoes and the crisp Indian snacks she would make for them.

Geetika was impressed at the conviction teenagers had these days. It was such a change from her adolescence. She remembered how, even at the cusp of adulthood, she would unquestioningly follow the choices others made for her.

For her fifteenth birthday last week, Uma had wanted a new, expensive watch. A volunteering stint at a local hospice had earned her the few dollars she had been short of. Geetika remembered what a contrast her own sixteenth birthday had been. All she had wanted was a badminton racquet. Her father, dismissing the request as a trivial one, had ordered an emerald necklace instead. Expensive and exquisite, it was a gift befitting a royal heiress, he had said. Disappointed, Geetika had canvassed her grandmother.

"Rani ma, I want to play badminton. What will I do with all these necklaces and earrings that mother keeps putting away for me in that big chest of hers?"

She had prepared herself for the matriarch's anger.

Instead, the old lady had laughed. "You are too much of a simpleton. In my time, my sisters and I would vie for our father's gifts. They were always jealous of me because I was the eldest princess and got the best gifts." Rani ma knew that these indulgences would be impossible for Geetika after she got married.

"Let the girl have whatever she wants. It is only a few years more before she leaves for the house that will be hers for life."

Too simple to think about the future or her grandmother's words, Geetika had been thrilled. As the memories came rushing now, she wondered what her granddaughters would think of her naivete.

Tara, at six, was talkative and chirpy. She loved rushing home to Geetika with stories of her day. Every night, Geetika would tell her a story, making it up as she went along. Tara would stop her by saying, "Grandma, tell me the one about the princess; Tara the princess." Geetika would then weave a story from her own past but put Tara at its centre. She would describe the opulence, grandeur, and luxury she had been born into. All Tara wanted was to imagine herself as the princess. After a while, her eyelids weary with sleep, she would snuggle up closer and ask, "So, you were a *real* princess?" And Geetika would reply, "Yes, my love. And so are you. Sleep well." Then she would sing the girl a traditional lullaby in her soft, lilting voice. The melodious song had been in their family for generations. Even though she couldn't understand the words, Tara loved the soothing tune. Geetika would continue to sing until the girl fell into a deeper sleep. She would gently drape the comforter on the little girl's curled-up body. Then, she would continue to hum as she walked back to her room, thinking of how she had sung the same song to her children years ago.

She opened the curtains, and the grey of the outdoors seeped inside. Everything seemed pale and faded. The lump in her throat was still there. She wondered if she would choke on it. She bent down near the dresser to open the last drawer. This time, she heard Gaurav's voice reminding her that her bones had never completely recovered from the radiation. Removing the neatly folded shawls, she reached for the box. Hugging it close to her chest, she sat down on the bed.

Duct-taping the corners of the cardboard box had not been enough to preserve it once it had started coming apart. So, a few years ago, she had finally transferred the contents to this plastic box. The pictures of multi-coloured balls of wool made on the original box remained fresh in her memory though. Her hands trembled as she removed the lid. She reached for the bundle of long airmail envelopes and blue inland letters. The postage stamps were colourful and diverse in their graphic art, representing the country's evolution over the decades. The postmarks, from civilian and army post offices, were smudged. Her name and address were neatly handwritten on each letter.

The letters didn't show any signs of age, other than a slight yellow discolouration on some of them. The paper knives she had always used ensured that the envelopes had been slit open neatly. She would carefully take out each letter she received and unfold it slowly. Having read it, she would then linger for a moment before putting it away. The box would remain unopened until the next letter arrived, which could be months or even years later. She had never needed to read any of them more than once.

She opened the letter that was at the bottom of the pile. The familiar scrawl stared up at her from the yellowed sheet. The words felt soft, like the creases she thumbed over.

3

"Dear Geetu,

It is difficult to believe that it has only been a month since I left college. The preparations for my joining the Academy seem to have extended beyond my home, to the entire village! Everyone is fussing over me, as if I have won a prize!

I need to keep reminding myself of the fact that mere selection to the hallowed portals of the National Defence Academy is not enough. After all, this is not the end of a dream; it is just the beginning. Mother, of course, will hear none of this. She is feeding me, as she must have when I was a toddler, and I find the kitchen always buzzing with activity. I have spent hours poring over the railway timetable with her, explaining the long journey from our tiny village to the Academy on the outskirts of Pune. While she is happy to learn about the salubrious climate there, she worries about the food. I shall end up carrying quite a lot of pickles and mathris!

I worry about leaving her alone. It is a measure of her strength that she has always encouraged this dream of mine. Not once did her hands tremble when she signed the forms for my admission. I can only hope to live up to the example of courage she has always set for me. I am grateful for the love and support of our village folk, who have been our family for many years now.

Other tasks have also kept me busy. Finally, my postal orders and certificates are in order, and the large black trunks have been painted with my name. I have begun to do the prescribed 40 push-ups and sit-ups every day, along with jogging circuits. I leave tomorrow, and I hope that I have attended to everything. Now, as I write to you, I'm beginning to feel slightly nervous. But later, tremendous excitement and enthusiasm will overwhelm me.

But enough about me! I am sure you are enjoying the new subjects in the second year. I must remind you of your promise to become a more vocal and active participant in the debating society and work towards keeping the flag of Vindhya House flying high."

∞

The long corridor of the college had been extremely crowded, and she had been overwhelmed. Students thronged the notice board to check the names of the 'houses' they had been allotted. She heard them murmur *Shivalik...Aravalli... Vindhya* as they extracted themselves from the crowd and peeled away. She had been unable to nudge her way from the back towards the list displayed on the notice board. As she stood there undecided, a lanky figure pushed his way past her and started moving towards the front. As people parted to make way for him, she took the opportunity and followed him.

"Vindhya," he spoke aloud. *Vindhya,* she whispered to herself and followed the stranger back into the corridor.

"You in Vindhya, too?" She had nodded.

"Vindhya meets in the amphitheatre at 2 pm," he said. "Thank you."

That left her with just enough time for a masala chai.

Masala chai. That was what the spunky kid behind the counter called the brew he was always making in his cauldron-like saucepan. He would boil the tea leaves till they were sapped of all their colour, throw in ginger, cardamom, cinnamon, and tulsi followed by considerable amounts of milk and sugar, and let the whole thing simmer for several minutes.

This saccharine-sweet drink was a contrast to the tea service she went home to every day. Her mother would place the little trolley in the lawns. The embroidered napkins would match the tea cosy. The teapot, the strainer with its holder, small jugs for milk, the sugar bowl with its tiny silver spoon—all of them were engraved with their family crest. Honey, freshly squeezed slices of limes, and salted nuts completed part of the evening ritual. Geetika would keep her books in her room and join her mother, and they would wait for her father.

Like for many other families, times had been changing for the erstwhile royal family of Kiratpur. Pradeep Kumar Singh had been an astute and foresighted ruler. He understood the changing paradigms of a newly independent India, and wanted his only child, Geetika, to be prepared for them. He had been appointed the Rai Bahadur of his erstwhile kingdom, a reward for his accession to India. The privileges this gave him would be instrumental in finding a suitor for his only child.

4

A few days later, she had been watching the layer of *malai* frost over the steaming hot beverage, when she heard a booming voice from behind her.

"Chotu! *Chaar chai. Jaldi*!" (Chotu! Four cups of tea. Quickly!)

"Yes, bhaiya."

In a flash, the silence of the cafeteria transformed into a buzz of chatter and activity.

At 6 feet 2 inches, Shekhar's lanky frame and long legs stretched out on the chair opposite his as he devoured his tea and samosa. His confidence and swagger set him apart from the other students in his group. She could hear snatches of their conversation which was loud but not boisterous. Their banter and obvious camaraderie held her attention.

She had listened silently as they spoke of Milkha Singh, Dilip Kumar's new movie, and Kishore Kumar's songs.

She saw him again at the debate club meeting the following Friday. It was her father who had insisted she try debating. Inherently shy, she remained, for many months, the quietest member of the club. Unlike Shekhar. His tall, lanky frame and his voice booming from the speaker made him impossible to miss.

That day, his eloquent speech about the space race between the United States and the Soviet Union had held everyone's attention. "So, what do think of the new agency the United States is establishing for space exploration?" he had asked as he slid into the vacant seat next to her. She had read about the National Aeronautics and Space Administration (NASA) in the newspapers. Not giving her a chance to reply, he had expanded on his own enthusiastic argument to include the Soviet Union, the moon, and Mars.

She had smiled.

"Oh! Sorry. I haven't introduced myself. I am Shekhar. First year."

As he looked askance at her, she sensed his unspoken question and said, "Geetika." Unsure about taking his outstretched hand, she had continued, "First year."

"Haven't heard you speak yet."

She gave him a half-smile, but kept silent, a little self-conscious.

They had walked out together, towards the library, before he rushed off to meet his friends. "Bye!" he called out.

They didn't have any subjects in common. She was studying Hindi and Home Science; he had chosen Science and English. But they found themselves together at the daily assembly and assorted events. The quiet observer and the eloquent speaker were drawn to each other. Her reticence didn't stop Shekhar from chattering constantly. If anything, his constant volley of observations, his laughter, and his mischief made her feel relaxed.

Shekhar was a star student. His confidence on the stage and public speaking skills ensured that he was at the forefront of every activity. But, despite his mini celebrity-like status, he would put everyone at ease. Friendly and amiable, he was endearing in his simplicity. Her consistent academic performance, graceful personality, and melodious voice (in which she would recite the college prayer every morning) had not gone unnoticed, either. No event in college was possible without them. The morning assembly, where she sang the invocation, always began with his testing the PA system, and ended with his vote of thanks.

After classes, they would catch up in the cafeteria over masala chai. Their many contrasts would be obvious even in this mundane activity. She would find it too sweet and milky, while he would ask for extra sugar and enjoy the layer of *malai* tickling his lips. She would help him rehearse and time his speech for the next debate. He would plead with her to sing a few lines of the latest Geeta Dutt songs.

Both would look forward to the second—and sometimes, third cup of tea—as much as to their long chats and light repartee.

One day, they had been sitting under the peepal tree, studying and making notes on the margins of their textbooks.

"You know, you are the reason I will soon be poor." Their eyes had met.

Hers were questioning, searching for the meaning of this remark.

His were shining with their trademark twinkle.

Holding her gaze, he had continued, "The Indian Government has introduced a new tax. On speaking. Since you don't speak at all, *I* am forced do all the talking. And I will be poor because of the high tax I will have to pay."

She had laughed out loud. A warm, joyous laugh that began deep inside her and spread cheer to everything around. And, for the first time in his memory, he was rendered speechless, as if spellbound.

Every day, they would sit with each other, catching up on lessons. They would linger in the amphitheatre after the House meeting, chatting about their day. She would sit beside him, her petite frame in a pastel-coloured saree. The diamond hoops that encased her earlobes would dance in the sunshine as she gently sipped her tea to the accompaniment of his slurps. The clasp of the tiny gold watch she wore would shine on her delicate wrist. Her tiny hands would push away the wisps of brown hair. Her eyes, with an ocean of kindness in them, would look across at him.

But that day, when she had laughed, it was different. If something could be the summer rain and the warmth of the winter sun at the same time, it was her joyous laughter. Decades later, it would continue to echo in his imagination—crystal clear, sparkling, and uplifting.

That moment, he had fallen in love with her. He felt as if he had stumbled upon a part of himself, a part he hadn't even known was missing. As if something he had been yearning for, without even being aware of it, had homed in and settled irreversibly in his soul.

Tea over, they had made their way to their respective classrooms. He had taken her hands in his, gently squeezed those delicate fingers and then released them.

"Bye!"

She had watched him stride off towards the laboratory. She knew she would see him again in a few hours, yet she waited until he was out of sight, and then some more.

That was when she had fallen in love with him.

It felt as if he had taken a piece of her with him. A piece she hadn't known existed. A piece that had been hidden deep within her, waiting to be found only by him. He had unearthed it, caressed it lovingly and tenderly, and walked away with it! It would now forever belong to him.

5

Each had never met anyone like the other before. Different backgrounds and divergent futures made them an unlikely couple. Yet, they felt that they belonged to and with each other—as if they had never been apart even before joining college.

As a toddler, Shekhar would decorate wooden toys with the Indian flag and pretend that they were army trucks. The one-room school in his tiny village of Lakhanpur had not been big enough for his dreams. Inspired by the stories of his father, a naib subedar in the Indian Army during the Burma War, he had decided that to live and die for his motherland was his calling. He had finished school, only to discover that he was too young to take the National Defence Academy (NDA) entrance examination that year. It was a temporary impediment, he told himself as he cycled the 7 km distance to college every day. A college that was to be his stepping stone to NDA. A college where he would bide his time before heading out to his real destination.

On his way back from college, he would stop to pick up firewood. Once home, he would help with the chores and help the children from the neighbourhood with their lessons. He would study late into the night, devouring his college books and preparing for the NDA exam. Like his teachers at school had, his professors at college also recognised his spirit and potential. There was no doubt that he would succeed in whatever he set his mind to.

Geetika had attended school on the palace grounds. Women in her family were usually married off in their teens. But times were changing. Her father understood that his daughter would lead a hugely different life, and that higher education was essential. Monarchy was abolished, but they were still bound by conventions and traditions. He decided that, at the right time, he would search for a man with whom his daughter could lead the life of privilege she had been groomed for. Meanwhile, she became the first woman in her family to attend college. Going to college was the first time she had had the days to herself, without a chaperone or a private tutor. It was a welcome change from the cloistered environment of her private school. She quickly began to enjoy the classes and the independence of college life. In the evening, she would return home to her mother and spend hours learning royal recipes, home remedies and embroidery, skills that her position in society would demand from her.

Joining college should not have been part of destiny's plan for either of them. Yet, that was where they had found themselves—and each other.

He had seen struggle and poverty, but they hadn't affected his positivity and zest for life. Her sheltered upbringing as a princess had kept her protected from many a reality but hadn't spoiled her.

Shekhar was a maverick who wanted to test all limits and challenge all rules. His teachers wondered how he would serve under the strict discipline of the armed forces. Geetika was the only one who realised his tremendous spirit. Only big challenges could quell the unrest he carried within him. He was meant to storm enormous bastions, never to be satisfied with small playing fields. It was with Geetika that his restlessness gave way to a calming and sobering stillness. Her serenity and composure brought him a sense of completeness. For Shekhar, she was Geetika the person, not a princess or an heir. And with him, she could be a simple girl unencumbered by protocol or hierarchy. His presence gave her the confidence to voice her emotions. Few people realised the clarity of thought and steely resolve that the petite, protected ex-princess possessed. He was struck by how her privileged life had not dimmed her compassion and humility. In turn, she was touched by the stories of his village and family. He encouraged her to join the social work wing of their college. The acumen she showed there in helping the women of the neighbouring villages become independent had been unexpected but not surprising.

Stolen glances turned into stolen moments. As the weeks passed, they would look for opportunities to be together. They cherished the hours spent in the library or the canteen, the long walks and the discreet trips to the city. Holding hands, they would disappear into the wilderness behind the college. The annual college excursion to a forest reserve introduced them to a passion and intimacy which they would never know with anyone else.

If fate hadn't scripted this year in their lives, their paths would probably never have crossed even in many lifetimes. But it did. And, they fell in love, as only soulmates can.

The year of college that had brought them together was coming to an end, as they had known it would. Shekhar's lifelong dream had come true, and he had been accepted into NDA. It was his last week in college. Their last week together.

"Geetu, I love you."

"I love you too, Shekhar."

They had hugged each other tightly.

"I wish we could be together."

"Why can't we, Shekhar?"

"You know why, Geetu. Because you are royalty, and my poor, village background makes me unworthy of your family."

"There is no royalty anymore. We are also common people now."

"Yes, but even then, the gap between us is too much. I don't think your family will ever agree to our match."

"You will be an officer in the Army, soon."

"Geetu, listen. If you feel that your father will agree to your waiting until I complete my course and am commissioned, I will accompany you right now and ask for your hand in marriage. To be able to spend my life with you is the only thing I really want, and I am willing to do whatever you ask me to do."

She had fallen silent. He was right. Her parents had become active in their search for an alliance for her. They were corresponding with other erstwhile princely states in search of someone whose stature matched theirs. The conversations at home only centred around how, after losing the kingdoms, lands, and royal titles, all that the family and her father had to fall back on was their reputation and prestige. And how, it was up to Geetika to ensure that these remained untarnished. Almost every day, her mother would remind her of the confidence they had placed in her by allowing her to attend college. Betrayal of this trust would not go down well with her father at all.

Her relationship with Shekhar would never be acceptable to her parents. Not now, not later.

"Geetu, we can either thank the universe for bringing us together and allowing us to know the joy of a connection as deep as ours; or we can resent life for not allowing us to drink more from this infinite ocean of love. Let us try and overcome the resentment and find courage in what we have experienced in these brief months."

She had buried her head in his chest, and he had nestled his chin on her head.

6

"Geetu, the Academy is everything I ever dreamt of! The uniform of a cadet is a privilege and an honour. Seeing myself in the uniform strengthens my will to succeed in the Academy and serve the nation. The rigorous courses are designed to strengthen us physically and mentally. Combat training is everything—and yet nothing—as I imagined it to be. I always knew it would take a lot of courage and strength, but the terms 'discipline' and 'concentration' have taken on new meaning now. Professionalism and dedication are embedded deep in the ethos of the Indian armed forces, and I hope to live up to these."

The Academy, spread over more than 6,000 acres, was as awe-inspiring as the list of cadets who had passed through its hallowed portals. The pink sandstone structure, with its lush green environs and the Sinhagad Fort standing tall against the clear blue skyline behind it, had left him captivated. Queuing up with other cadets, he had felt as if he had awakened from a dream. And a dream this had indeed been, for as long as he could remember. He had renewed his commitment to the nation and earnestly begun his training.

And she? She had slipped his letter into a book, to take it with her to college. Over small sips of milky chai, she had savoured each word of the letter again and again. Of course, he would be the best cadet of his batch. He would succeed in whatever he put his mind to. The cadet's uniform would be replaced by the officer's uniform, and later, that would be decorated by many medals. There was no doubt in her mind that, with soldiers as committed and capable as he, the country was in safe hands.

"Dear Geetu,

So you leave college, our college, behind and enter the next phase of your life!

I wonder how you will look in the garb of a bride. And then I decide that it does not matter. Whatever bridal finery you choose for this day cannot enhance your beauty and radiance. It is not the without that makes you shine; it is the within. Timeless beauty and purity of the heart and soul are what you embody, and these need no embellishment. That said, I am sure you will look royal and magnificent, as befits a queen.

I wish you all the very best for all time to come."

A suitor had been found.

The large province of Kiratpur to which Geetika belonged, was separated from the groom's family estate in Pratapgarh by the rugged terrain of the mountains, and a few customs and traditions. Maharaja Vikramjeet Singh had held out on the accession to India as long as possible. But now, the province would be integrated into the new state of Himachal Pradesh. And Geetika, into Vikram's family.

The trousseau had been carefully selected. Only the best of silks and brocades, with threads of gold and exquisite weaving, could accompany the bride. The most precious stones were sourced from distant states. Emeralds, rubies, polki, and diamonds would come together in tasteful, hand-crafted pieces. And there was no one better than her mother Rudrani Devi to ensure this. Many a jeweller failed the scrutiny to which she subjected their wares. Geetika had inherited her mother's tastes and sensibilities. Mother and daughter worked to design the ornate and precious pieces of bridal jeweller.

The arrangements had to be in keeping with the status of royals. The customs of both families would be honoured. In earlier days, Geetika's father would have ordered the release of prisoners and declared a holiday in his kingdom to celebrate her wedding. But now, as Rai Bahadur, he would organise an event everyone would remember for its splendour. This would be the last event in the haveli, the last royal wedding, and it would have to live up to the expectations of grandeur everyone had from the nobility.

Erstwhile kings, industrialists, ministers, and even movie stars had graced the ceremonies. The haveli was done up with sheer organza curtains, the finest upholstery, and shimmering lights. Colourful flower decorations offset the shining white marble. The wedding feast served more than 500 guests. The tables were decked with fancy goblets, plates, and spoons. The family's signature curries were made from the finest ingredients. Filigree gold leaves covered the mithai.

The cold weather and rough terrain meant that the groom could be accompanied by only a few of his family members. The rest of the large family had stayed back, waiting to welcome the bride in their sprawling estate.

"So, the young prince isn't coming on a horse, after all! The long limousine is a contemporary alternative, and much more suited for your royal persona. I must say it is a very exclusive choice. May it transport you to the palace that will bring you the comforts and fortune you have been born for!"

A few elderly men folk had accompanied Vikramjeet, the bridegroom. The polio-afflicted groom hadn't been able to mount a horse at the wedding function, and had to be helped by a few people.

It is a rare marriage that starts off on a perfect note, Geetika's family had murmured. Adjustment and compromise by the bride had been the cornerstones of so many marriages over generations. And these were the values the princess of Kiratpur had been brought up with

"You must have settled into your new abode now. It is only natural to miss your home. And your large, warm, and loving family. I confess I too was homesick when I first came here. But, be assured, you will gradually get used to the new place and the unfamiliar faces. I know that your large-heartedness will compensate for this house being smaller than the one you are used to. And your elegance will compensate for the grandeur that is

missing. Your warmth will light up your home and everyone's lives. Do not fret over unforeseen circumstances. They are a part of our lives, and are what force us to discover our reservoirs of strength. Some relationships may take longer than others, but I am sure you will nurture each one of them. God willing, all uncertainties will slowly disappear."

The haveli had been in a dilapidated state. Vikramjeet's debt-ridden family had been unable to retrieve it from the mortgage. Melancholy had made its presence felt in every nook and corner of the building. The sorrowful environment was disheartening to the young, graceful princess. But she was expected to be an antidote for Vikramjeet's bitterness and a foil for his frustration.

Vikram would speak of his kingdom, subjects, and royal lifestyle all the time. A part of him still inhabited a world in the past. He had not reconciled himself to having to give up his royal status. Geetika's disbelief and disenchantment had hardened into anger when she had learned of Vikram's failed first marriage. But in a household full of strangers, there was no room for her anger to find release. Her new life had begun thus, with disillusionment and much trepidation.

Vikram's refusal to accept the reality of accession had proved very costly. His life, and hers, by extension, was an exercise in maintaining the façade of royalty. The privy purse was emptying faster than she could keep track. The lavish parties, the retinue of servants to wait upon him, the flashy automobiles he had customised for himself and the polo team that he captained from the stands were all pretences that she found tiresome. She would entreat him to reconcile himself with the present and plan for the future. But he was unable to break free from the shackles of his grand past. As much as he tried to flaunt his royal lineage, she began to resent it. *Would peace and happiness remain elusive forever?* she wondered.

7

Motherhood had brought her joy, but also uncertainty. So precious he had been, her frail baby; his skin a soft shade of brown, and his hair a curly mop. She had held him close to her chest and felt a love she had never imagined. Vikram had insisted on naming him after his father, in the royal tradition. "Our kingdom has always celebrated the birth of an heir. We must distribute gifts to the entire estate. You worry too much. Gopal will change our fortunes, Maharani!"

Heir to what? What circumstances would he grow up in? she had wondered.

"Why do you worry about naming your child according to others' wishes? He is yours. He will always hear your voice and respond to whatever your heart chooses to call him. I see you nod your head and wonder how I know this when I have no experience with these matters. I know because I too have a mother like you, strong but tender. And I know that the children of such mothers will always be close to their hearts. A mother's love is a strange thing, Geetu! It is soft and gentle, but at the same time, fierce. It is infinite, and so is the strength it brings along. So, cherish the little one."

Gopal's frequent bouts of sickness, and his shy and sensitive nature, kept her preoccupied. She would silently watch Vikram dress up Gopal with a ceremonial turban on his head. She would cringe when he would pretend to tutor the toddler in the etiquette of the royal durbar. The flamboyance of his father on a good day, alternating with the oppressive silence on a bad one, taught Gopal to mind his actions and words. It had also made him more attuned to his mother's feelings and, later, her pain.

Slowly, he withdrew from his father and drew closer to his mother.

∞

"My pleasure and pride at finally being commissioned as an officer of the Indian Army are immense. Even more so, because my mother, frail and nervous but gleaming with happiness, was able to witness the realisation of this dream. She was beside herself with joy when I was awarded the Gold Medal for being the best cadet in the Academy.

Now, as the euphoria has died down, I prepare to move to my first posting, far away in South India. It feels a little strange! On the one hand, it feels that I was born in this uniform. And, on the other, I am aware every moment that this is a privilege, an honour, to be earned and cherished. Are these two not conflicting feelings? I can imagine you smiling and telling me not to complicate this special occasion."

You are right, I must stop rambling about this. The training ends, but the real journey begins now. So, this moment, and all that it means, will be one of the best memories of my life."

As the finances dried up, Vikram's extravagance and his drinking had increased. Geetika would temporarily pacify the moneylenders by handing over some expensive artifacts or paintings to them. But she wondered how long this would last. Families like theirs were a drain on the developing and emerging nation. *Daak* from the government offices reiterated that the future of the princely allowance was uncertain. She would plead with Vikram to explore other sources of income.

"But what will people say? That Maharaja Vikram Singh had to resort to selling his wife's jewels?" he had thundered on those occasions.

"A king never deserts his subjects." The thought of giving up his estate hadn't gone down well with him.

Finally, the idea of a car museum had appealed to his vanity. "Everyone will appreciate the grandeur of my kingdom." Vintage cars were his passion. He would enjoy being driven around in the shiny beauties, with little Gopal on his lap. With an economy of money and an extravagance of creativity and effort, Geetika had set up the museum. She had hoped this would give Vikram a new direction and help him turn over a new leaf.

But their visions were at odds. His indulgence would jumpstart a new, lavish life. The slow, uninteresting life of heading out from home to his office wasn't for him. He was born for the fast pace of life that his shiny sedans symbolised. He was forever making grandiose plans to have new cars customised for himself, renovate the garages and hire new staff.

His disinterest in the mundane had meant that she would have to step up. She had started corresponding with vintage car rally organisers to rent their cars. Money had begun to trickle in. Vikram's drinking bouts had decreased. She had allowed herself to believe they could be a family with stability and a future.

For some time Vikram had shown interest in his new way of life, but that proved to be an illusion. His priority had been different. He had wanted to fight the Indian Government for his privy purse. The income from the museum could not be put to better use, could it? Geetika had winced when he had signed away an entire month's allowance in a flash and handed the cheque over to the lawyer who was representing him in the suit against the Indian government.

The parallel universe he inhabited was so removed from their real world. He could identify with nothing but being a monarch. Being a husband, a partner or a parent was too trivial in his scheme of things. And being a commoner was unfathomable!

He would be consumed by the alcohol that had become his sustenance. Drunk, he would forget to strap on the caliper on his polio-afflicted leg, and stumble. His anger at not being helped immediately would be targeted at the glass in the chandeliers and windows. Then he would sit beside her and, speech slurring, ramble about his past grandeur. Oblivious to his scared son who would hide trembling behind Geetika, he would turn aggressive and demand more alcohol. He would be deaf to his wife's pleadings. The wife he called Rani Geetika Devi even in their most intimate moments.

These realisations had numbed Geetika. And a crushing loneliness had become part of her.

8

"Geetu, Geetu, Geetu....

I could write your name a hundred times over. Because each time I do it, I can see your face and feel the tranquillity I desperately need. Yes, the restless part of me refuses to be quelled even by the long sprints and exhausting swimming laps that I must keep doing. Why do I feel this way, you ask? It looks certain that war will happen. What is killing me right now is the uncertainty regarding my role in it. As you know, the enemy is making inroads daily into the land I have sworn to protect. Meanwhile, I am posted far away from our borders. It is frustrating to be so far away from the action. What if the opportunity to fight for my homeland slips away from my hand, as so much that is dear to me always has?

Mother was not keeping well, so I am home for a few days. I find myself taking long treks through the mountains. Perhaps I do this to distract myself from her failing health. She is insisting on me getting married. She has collected some photographs sent by doting fathers! Some come with promises of grand functions, while others speak of gifts. How do I explain that I do not want these presents or displays?

I can see you smile. I hear you say that the rituals can be simple, but that I should consider finding a partner to share my life with.

Geetu, for the first time in all these years, I will confess something to you. This bravado, this devil-may-care attitude that the world sees in me, is a façade. You laugh! Of course, you saw through it years ago, but I had hoped (and still do) that no one else will."

She smiled, just as she had when she had received the letter. Except that there had been no lump in her throat then.

"This talk of marriage makes me, a soldier trained for combat, nervous. I have never understood what my company will offer someone. Will someone who has only seen my photograph come out of a small yellow envelope ever be able to understand me? Will she know what drives me, what moves me, what angers me? And, how can the description of being of fair complexion and having big eyes tell me if she will be able to identify with my calling? How well she can cook seems to be irrelevant to me, compared with what she will make out of my nomadic existence. Those smiles I see in their photos—eager, tentative or hopeful—will I be able to protect them from the tests that life will bring?

I can tell that you are not impressed with my argument. Well, neither was my mother. And she has refused to let me off the hook. She keeps assuring me that understanding and patience go a long way in any relationship. Love too will follow as time passes. This, I confess, confused me. 'How can we know whether love will happen or not? Or where we will find it?' I tried to reason with her.

But my mother, as you might have realised, is not a woman who is easily convinced. Cornered, I finally confessed. I told her that I had fallen in love. She was immediately happy for me. Sitting beside her, holding her hand, I began to answer the questions she hadn't asked.

'Mother, you know that I always wanted to be a soldier. Training at the Academy was my biggest dream; nothing could stop me from fulfilling it.'

She nodded, and I continued. 'College, which I attended for a year, was just a stepping stone to my big plans. Little did I know how small the plans we make for ourselves are in the face of life, fate, and destiny. Mother, that year in college, I fell in love! So deep was this feeling that I could have even given up my dream to become a soldier! If it meant that I could attain this love, I would have agreed to part with everything dear to me. Gentle, demure, and kind, she was the most beautiful person to have walked this Earth. Her laughter would bring me joys I hadn't known existed. She was everything I had ever imagined a soulmate to be, and much more. It was as if I had been only half alive until then, and the rest of me had been waiting to be awakened. And such a soft, gentle awakening it was!

Her hands tousling my wavy and rebellious hair; my head in her lap as we talked for hours; her hands in mine; her grip on my waist as we bicycled into town. Surely, this was enough to live for and die for? I discovered that, in love, each moment can be a lifetime. And a lifetime of togetherness was what we found with each other. Those moments were so precious to us that we couldn't allow them to be tarnished by the reality that our love would be unrequited.'

Mother asked me then what it was that stopped me from making my dream come true. It wasn't like me to give up without trying, she said. After all, I have never stopped short of pursuing anything I set my mind to, have I? Such is the faith mothers have in their children, Geetu! Or perhaps, it pains them to see their child lose something they are so attached to?

I was at a loss for words. I asked her to get some sleep.

What else could I have done, Geetu? How could I tell her that it had all been a dream? That dreams could be real and tangible, yet fragile and delicate at the same time? That love that seemed so powerful and strong could also be delicate and diaphanous? Would she have understood what I was telling her? Or had she already understood it without my ever saying it? With mothers, you never know what they carry deep in their hearts.

She slept. And it pleased me that it was a comfortable sleep; not the kind that was interrupted by shivers. I watched her frail chest rise and fall with her breathing, as she must have watched mine when I slept as a child. My rambling about the past is so very unlike me, no? I suppose my mother's emotions have rubbed off on me. Now, I must get some sleep. I return to the unit tomorrow. Most of my friends have received their orders; I await mine."

The newspapers had dutifully reported the build-up at the border. Staccato voices on the radio spoke about the movement of troops. She remembered the palpable tension and the threat of war as if it were just yesterday. Like her life, the timeline of the country seemed to be punctuated with turbulence.

That letter had been followed a few days later by a brief note.

∞

"The orders have come. We are moving tomorrow; I cannot tell you where to. This is the opportunity for which I have trained hard. It is both the chance and the responsibility of a lifetime. I hope I will not let down my mother, who bid me goodbye with her blessings; or my motherland, which has given me the privilege to defend her. I don't know when I will write to you next. You must always remember that adversity and turbulence will be temporary. Even in times of despair, your courage must keep shining through, showing you the way—as it always has."

The war had begun. She had been confident that the country was in good hands, with soldiers like Shekhar. But about her own life, she hadn't been so sure. She had devoted herself completely to the management of the car museum, even during her second pregnancy. Vikram kept the accounts, but she coordinated all the activities and the running of the museum. Gaurav's birth was followed by an unexpected victory.

"Maharani Geetika Devi, see what your husband is capable of! The accession was our nation's foolishness. Rajahs are those who can take tough decisions and fight for their rights. This trait runs in our blood. A group of people sitting and poring over books and running a country is a recipe for disaster. This democracy will not last long. Power will return to those its rightful heirs."

They had won the case. Pending payments had been released by the Indian government and she had been able to pay sundry creditors off. The allowance and the income from the museum would be enough for them to get by.

She began to feel the comfort that hope can bring. At least, briefly. Then the sudden amendment to the Constitution stopped all allowances and privileges to the erstwhile royals. They were ordinary citizens now, equal to other Indians, including the ones they had been born to rule over.

The joys Gaurav had brought into their lives had also been brief. After initial attempts at being a doting father, Vikram had begun to see the child as an heir without a kingdom. He became a reminder of all that Vikram had lost.

The erstwhile king had heard stories of other erstwhile royals entering politics. The democracy he had rubbished all along now seemed an attractive proposal.

"Kings don't plan for the future, Maharani. They make it." He was confident that the locals would support him in the elections. And he would rule again.

He had been wrong. Losing the election had meant the loss of face and money.

9

"Geetu, I have never felt so much pain. While I was defending my country, I lost my mother. As you can imagine, I am unable to express my sorrow. Another reason for my anguish is that I lost three men in battle. A good leader should sacrifice himself before his men, and I think I have failed them and their families. Seeing the horrors and carnage first-hand made me realise that there can be no winners in war. The award that the government has bestowed upon me feels underserved and this glory, shallow. I know you will understand how lost and unsure I feel.

I can imagine you telling me that I must go on. Yes, I must. And, I will! Hopefully, this cloud of gloom and dejection will not hover for long. After a struggle with myself, which can be far worse than a skirmish on the border, I have decided to accept the award and dedicate it to those who sacrificed themselves. It is what my mother would have wanted me to do."

∞

The last of the sycophants had finally disappeared. It was just the four of them now. For a while, Vikram remained sober enough to confront reality. She convinced him to allow the banks to auction some of their properties. They would buy back the haveli and continue running the museum, she said. She would watch Gopal walk to school wearing the light brown uniform, his books in a cloth bag, like all the other children. *His life was so different from her lavish childhood,* she would think. Then she would remind herself that, at least, they finally had some stability in life.

But she couldn't help noting how Vikram's garrulous nature resulted in disagreements with the bank officials.

His arrogance ensured that they returned empty from the negotiating table. He seemed intent on self-destructing. She could feel the grip she had carefully kept on everything beginning to slip.

But even the foreboding that all was not well hadn't been enough to prepare her for what was to come next.

10

"I am deeply saddened by this news and wonder how much more trouble is written in your destiny. I will not ask you how you are coping. I can tell you that I can try to feel your pain, but even that will be of little consolation. I feel wretched that I am unable to help you. I pray that you find the tremendous reserve of strength that is hidden in your delicate frame. I beg of you: please do not surrender to the despair and desolation that is threatening to envelop you."

She couldn't let the tears fall on the paper. She had reached for a handkerchief.

The headline in the newspapers had screamed:

Erstwhile prince crashes car. Was probably inebriated

The new sedan had been customised just recently. They would often go out in the evenings, the four of them. Driving was the only thing that made Vikram feel in control of himself and his life. Gopal would enjoy sitting in the front seat, listening to his father explain the car's controls. Geetika would be happy to have the backseat, with Gaurav playing in her lap.

That evening, however, Vikram had stepped out alone. He had taken the car for a spin on the highway, where the newly laid roads and signposts announced the developing economy and the progress of the country. A dispossessed prince with a fondness for alcohol and his shiny new vehicle made a lethal cocktail. It was perfect material for the tabloids. Their reports gave the reader an opportunity to pronounce judgment on Vikram's character and discuss the cycle of karma. Who would ever know that it had been one of the rare evenings when Vikram hadn't been drinking; that a deal with Daimler for the museum had seemed promising and that they had spent that afternoon like a regular, close-knit family?

Their lives and their truths would soon be forgotten. The three of them would have to pick up the scattered pieces of their lives and rearrange them to give them a new form. It would be many years—or decades—later that they would arrive at their respective truths regarding the events of that fateful evening. Would the boys equate the bad decisions made by their father with his being a bad *person*? Would they be harsh on him in their memories? How different would their realities be from hers?

She had reconciled herself to the opinion that Vikram had been an unfortunate product of his circumstances. The loss of the only identity that had ever meant anything to him—that of a ruler, a rajah, a king—had made it impossible for him to identify with any of the other roles life gave him a chance at. Husband, manager, father or entrepreneur—he had never been able to own those roles. If the monarchy hadn't been abolished, or if he had had the capacity to accept change gracefully, he would have been a different person. And they would have led vastly different lives. But life is the sum of choices. And often, the choices in one's life are made by someone else.

At that moment, dwelling on these things was a luxury for Geetika. As was allowing herself to be overcome by grief.

11

Vikram's disinterest in anything pragmatic was reflected in the bank accounts. The debt was more than she had expected. Notices from the banks were piling up. She recalled the large durbars, where her father would write off loans taken by many of his subjects. His magnanimity had been appreciated. Yet, it had also diminished its recipient. And now that she was in their place, she understood the shadow of embarrassment she had seen on those relieved faces. In spite of that, she would have been relieved to have found a benefactor now. But there was none.

The haveli would be auctioned by the bank. A good price was expected, and she might be able to buy back a part of the estate. The museum had become popular with tourists, but the cost of maintaining the cars was mounting. *Difficult times were never ended by taking the easy way out*, she could imagine her father say. The aristocratic life had given her a wondrous and joyful childhood. But it had also led her into a strained marriage and a tarnished future. Vikram had tried to fight fate—and lost. Stories of their royal life had to be consigned to history now. Their past should not obstruct their future.

She would severe all her connections with the erstwhile royalty. She wondered how Gopal and Gaurav would feel about this decision. Would they feel later that she should have tried to salvage some vestige of their royal life? Did they not deserve to know these parts of themselves? Would they judge her for this irrevocable step later? But even if they did, she hoped it wouldn't be too harshly.

"Geetu, I am not sure if there are any correct or incorrect decisions in situations like this. And, I don't say this merely to

placate your anxiety. Not just others, we ourselves will often judge the choices we made. I have struggled a lot, wondering if I did the right thing that fateful night in the battle. Should I have ordered the men to return to the post? Had there been enough time to wait for reinforcements while trying to capture the crucial bunkers? Each time I struggled with these questions, the answers that came to mind were different. My mind would incessantly think of so many possibilities over which I had no control then, or later. It was a consistent reminder that we will never know if what we are doing is right or wrong. The only thing we will know is that it feels like the best possible option. We must do what needs to be done: whatever seems right at that moment in time. And, we must trust that we will be strong enough to bear the consequences of our decisions."

She met the accountants to discuss the ledgers. For each credit entry they made, expenses or debts already existed. But she persisted. She redid the calculations. She studied bank deposit rates and hypothecation papers. She revisited her Accounts classes from her college days and immersed herself in the figures. She wrote to business scions who could give her a good price for the vintage vehicles. She telegrammed Bellagio and Chrysler and Daimler to buy back the beauties for their corporate museums. She permitted the bank to auction the remaining paintings, antiques, and sculptures, along with the land and estate.

12

The tempo had been loaded with the sparse belongings that remained. The taxi was ready to take them to their new—and much humbler—home. It was just a few kilometres away from the erstwhile royal estate, but it seemed like another world. She had not looked back on her life as the princess of Kiratpur when she had arrived here, and she would not look back on the phase of her life she was leaving now.

Gaurav playfully jumped and skipped as they walked out of the haveli's gates for the last time. Gopal looked back over his shoulder at the home in which he had spent too many years of his life to forget easily.

It was a warm day, typical of the bright summer afternoons of the mountains. Yet, she had shivered. As if a bitter, cold wind was penetrating her bones and not allowing her to move. What would the future bring? She had clasped her children's hands in hers and stopped in her tracks. And suddenly, the shivering had stopped. She had felt warm and calm, as if someone or something was reaching out to her, reassuring her that she would be able to deal with whatever came her way.

Head held high, she led the boys away from the gates of the house she had entered as a bride many years ago.

"New beginnings are seldom what they seem, Geetu. Nor is it possible, sometimes, to differentiate a beginning from an end. Such is the cycle of life. Aah, there is a tiny furrow on your forehead as you wonder why I am talking in riddles.

Well, I need you to be sitting down before you read any further about the developments in my life. And there have been quite a few of them! However much you may prepare yourself, you will never be able to guess what I am about to tell you. Geetu, I am now a married man, hahahaha!

I can see that soft, tender smile. I can also imagine the surprise you must be feeling at this sudden news. Let me begin at the very beginning.

You will remember how I told you, all those years ago, that our home was different from all the others in the village. I would observe how my mother never adorned my father's picture with the marigold necklace. She would lovingly caress the glass when she cleaned it each morning. The pain of living a life of uncertainty affected her more than she ever showed. Not knowing if my father, who had gone to war when she had been a young bride, was captured, lost or dead must have been unbearable for her. But she never complained. That is the way it is with women who are strong and courageous: like my mother, you, and the woman with whom I now share my life.

You know that my mother had been insistent on the matter of my marriage. Yet, she had let me play truant from becoming a householder. I knew it was not the effect of my eloquent speech. There was something else holding her back. She could not bear another woman having to face the fate she had to; to live with the pain she had endured. The day I left home, I took blessings from my father's photograph and from her. Then I told her that she could look forward to conducting my wedding after I returned from the war. You will understand the unsaid words that would have hung in the air between us. Yet, brave woman that she was, there was not even a tiny tear in the corner of her eye as she hugged me and bid me goodbye.

I had never imagined that I would return to a home without my mother. But then, who has been able to foretell the future? And even if we could, we wouldn't have the strength to face it.

So now, with the blessings of the simple and loving people of my village, I have fulfilled the promise I gave my mother. This is how another strong woman, who did not have the luxury to mourn the death of her betrothed, became a part of my life. I will forever be grateful to her for agreeing to my proposal, which, I admit, I made rather shyly. I hope I can be worthy of her.

I did stick to my guns about not having a ceremony. After signing the papers at the registrar's office, we proceeded to the party at the officers' mess. I mustered up the courage to hit the dance floor after more than a decade. It will amuse you to learn that my dancing has not improved a wee bit! Clumsy and awkward as ever, I fear I made a fool of myself.

The other reason I write about beginnings and endings being indistinguishable from each other is that I know you are settling into yet another phase of your life. Yes, this life is different from the one anyone would ever have foreseen for you, but who are we to question fate? I pray that you see happier, easier, and simpler times than you have in the past."

The income from interest amounts and pension had not been enough to sustain the young widow with an incomplete college degree.

"Don't take things to heart. Life has to be lived. And, sometimes, we are hard-pressed for options. Pragmatism and matter-of-fact decisions, ignoring sentiment and emotion, are often needed. I am sure a woman as talented as you will be able to give a new perspective to selling the family silver. Besides, there is no gold or silver that is more valuable than love. And you have that in abundance."

She had opened Vikram's locker to find the expensive, ornate pieces of jewellery that had accompanied her as a bride. How zealously he had kept them tucked away, refusing to part with anything that reminded him of his royal status! She had never had the occasion to wear the expensive pieces and couldn't imagine a future in which she would. These ornaments were what she would turn to in her dire times. She returned to her notebooks and made a list of all the jewels and the stones that had been carefully collected by her parents and passed on to her.

The lands her father had willed to her had been sold by Vikram. She recalled her visit to the hospital, when her father had been on his deathbed, his face ashen and guilt-ridden. *"I would never have imagined that things would come to this, beta,"* he had said. She had wiped his tears—and her own—and asked him to rest. The money he had left her from his allowance as Rai Bahadur had been enough to pay off a few loans. But, over the years, the corpus he had left for her got exhausted, even the amounts he had presented to Vikram on the birth of both her children.

Only these jewels remained, shimmering solutions to her woes. She would sell them gradually, planning her expenses and budget carefully. There were many years—and responsibilities—ahead of her. Thankfully, the quality of the stones was unmatched, and she was rediscovering her flair for design. She began to think beyond the obvious step of selling the stones and pieces to wholesalers. Royal jewellery styles were in vogue and commanded a good price in the retail market. She would reset the pieces she was selling into simpler and smaller but unique ones. These elegant, regal, and functional pieces would be appreciated. Dealers would return to her with specific requests.

She didn't realise it then, but these were the first tentative steps of *Ranima Ki Potli.*

13

"Geetu!

In all the years I have known you, I have never felt angry with you! But today, I wonder why you never told me about the pure joy that becoming a parent can bring. Yes, I have a little daughter! It has been only three days since I first held her in my arms, fearful of dropping her or damaging her fragile frame. But it feels like she has been with me from a previous life. I hope I am competent enough to protect this little gift of God. May she become strong enough to be able to hear her own voice and follow her heart.

I know it has been long since I wrote to you. I have been busy with my discharge from the army. I can feel your surprise, and it is not unwarranted. I can also imagine the questions that must be arising in your mind. I will answer some of them.

The difficult time after the war was made even more so by the fact that mother was no more. As you know, the intensive firing had injured me. Recovery was slow, and the results of the surgeries were disappointing. It seemed like the mental agony and physical pain would last a lifetime. Or at least, their scars would. The love of those around me made my convalescence easier and I was able to put much of the traumatic flashbacks behind me. But, while time does heal, sometimes, the healing is not complete. That is what happened with me, too.

Everything was the same but felt different. I found myself fretful at first, then resentful and even frustrated. I could feel those emotions singeing everything I touched. So, after much deliberation, I sought discharge from the forces. Do not worry; I am not at all despondent. I know I have served my country and countrymen well. I was fortunate to have got the opportunity to do so. As no one knows better than you, we must accept what time has in store for us and try to make the best of it.

Just as you have succeeded in making your jewellery venture a success against all odds, I hope to make the best of my changing circumstances and not to dwell on what is no longer possible.

My new responsibilities extend beyond my being a parent. My country has chosen me to set up a new intelligence organisation called Indian Military Intelligence Organisation (IMIO), that will change the course of our defence strategies in the years to come. Military intelligence is something our country will need in future to deal with external and internal threats, and for developing our foreign policy. This assignment will bring opportunities to travel, learn and grow in ways that are new to me, and I have accepted the challenge with enthusiasm. And it is you, Geetu, who is my inspiration. Your immense strength and courage are reminders of how we can overcome even the most difficult situations with grace and equanimity."

She had known he would be successful in whatever he set out to do and would always serve the country. She said a silent prayer for his safety as she put the letter away.

Those years had been eventful for both of them. The new beginnings had slowly changed the fabric of their lives. The children and the business had kept her busy. And both showed the results of her efforts. He, on the other hand, had been travelling to different parts of the country, recruiting agents, raising covert forces and laying the building blocks of IMIO.

14

"Congratulations on Gopal's admission to engineering college! The young man has done very well in his studies, and I am sure he will continue to do so in life. Don't worry about him. He has learned from you how to make the best of every situation. Having a mother like you has given him enough confidence and fortitude to face any challenge. I am sure he will adjust well to this new phase of independence. It is interesting that you are travelling to Bangalore at around the same time that I will be there. I will be available at this number after 6 pm on all days of next month."

Gopal's admission procedures and her appointments with jewellers kept her occupied in Bangalore. Finally, all engagements taken care of, she had reached for the piece of paper on which she had carefully copied down the phone number.

There had been no answer. The next day, she had called again. This time it was answered, but without the customary 'Hello'.

"Geetu." He had said a single word.

Standing by the window in her hotel room, she had pressed the receiver into her face.

"Yes."

They had said nothing for a few moments. There was no static, either. Just silence. To which both of them had listened intently.

"Shall we meet tomorrow? 5 pm, Taj, MG Road?"

"Yes."

Two decades, and all of life's vagaries, had seemed to dissolve into nothing as he went to the Reception to receive her.

There was not a single strand of grey in her hair. Her glowing skin, those beautiful, deep-set, kohl-lined eyes and the pink lips that needed no gloss; she was as beautiful as she had always been. The grey pearl studs in her ears matched the pale grey embroidery in her pink flowing kurta. Fine lines around her eyes were the only reminder of all that she had gone through, but even these disappeared into the softness of her face. The printed dupatta she had wrapped around her face like a stole was the perfect frame for her tentative smile. She looked as ethereal as ever. Marriage, children, widowhood, life, scars—nothing had diminished her regal demeanour.

He had been as awestruck then, as he had been that day when she had burst into laughter in the college canteen. The pale green chiffon saree flowing, her hair loosely tied, the string of pearls adorning her neck—he could close his eyes and visualise that day even after all these years. He knew that these two images of her timeless beauty would remain frozen in his memory forever.

Wordlessly, he had led her to the coffee shop. They sat with each other, the circular table in front of them. The boyish gleam in his eyes, the waviness of his hair, his smell as she brushed against him when he pulled out the chair for her—nothing had changed.

He was wearing deep-blue trousers and a plain white shirt, but to her eyes, it felt like the soldier's uniform she would always imagine him in, despite never having seen him in one.

For many minutes, neither of them spoke. They just took in the distance life had put between them; a distance that seemed infinite yet non-existent. There might have been so much to say after so long. But there hadn't been. There might have been tears or laughter. But there hadn't been. There was a wholeness—a completeness—and the calm that it brought to both.

He had needed to touch her, to make sure this was happening; that she was here, with him. He gently put his right arm around her shoulder. She reached for his hand—and felt the limp sleeve of his shirt.

Her eyes welled up as she heard about his left hand getting blown to smithereens by the grenades. He told her of the surgeries that had followed, of the painful delirium, of the slow recovery. She felt the pain of knowing that all that he had ever wanted—to serve at the frontlines—was not to be anymore.

Wiping her tears away, he said, "This is nothing, Geetu. You know I would have given my life."

"You have also gone through so much," she whispered.

"Who hasn't? Haven't you gone through even more?" he said softly as he moved closer to her. "I wish I could have done even the slightest thing to make your life easier; that I could have reached out and comforted you in what must have been the most difficult moment of your life."

She looked at the teardrop at the corner of his eye. And, she understood. The afternoon she had been leaving the haveli, it was *his* presence she had felt. His presence that had stopped her from breaking down in the face of her tragedy and the uncertain future and given her the courage to step into the unknown with her little boys.

"You were there..."

"Yes, Geetu. I was returning to the Command Hospital in Delhi after my wedding. They would be attempting one more surgery; the last, they said. I couldn't stop myself from taking a detour to see you. But seeing you was all I could do. To reach out to you would have meant letting you see me at my weakest: injured, fatigued and beaten. Holding you might have broken you further. I felt truly helpless. It wasn't enough, but at least, I saw you."

"It was, Shekhar, it was."

And they had spoken on. About everything and nothing, of things close to their hearts and of matters that were of no consequence.

They sat for what seemed like days, unaware of the torrential rain, that stopped as suddenly as it had begun. Geetika caressed the stump of his left hand. Even over the rough scars, she felt only softness.

He didn't have to speak of the burdens that lay buried deep inside him and that caused his shoulders to droop. She instinctively knew how he would often find his head pounding and hear the sounds of shelling reverberate in his thoughts.

"Shekhar, it was not your fault. Those men you lost… there was nothing you could have done. You have to let it stop haunting you."

He didn't need to ask her how she knew of the one nightmare that still recurred, or of how the crippling anxiety incapacitated him even as he trained agents in espionage.

He sighed. At least now, finally, the nightmares, the sounds and the pain would begin to fade away, he hoped.

Shekhar kept his right arm around her, occasionally pushing back the loose tresses of hair that fell on her face. The moon rose and then set, giving way to the sun again, but they remained in the 24-hour coffee shop. Half-nibbled sandwiches and tall glasses of orange juice with melted ice cubes witnessed their connection, deep as ever.

It was dawn when he returned to his quarters in the cantonment area. The letter from headquarters that he had received yesterday, pertaining to IMIO, was on his desk. Watching the drizzle fall on the lush greenery outside, he reached for the letter he had written just before leaving to meet Geetika. Just last evening, not even 24 hours ago, he had decided to decline the offer to take operational charge of the company and run it, even though he himself had founded it. Because he had felt unworthy of the role.

He now tore the letter into a hundred pieces and tossed them into the wastepaper basket. Reaching for a fresh sheet of paper, he wrote his reply, accepting the position.

Back in her hotel room, she carefully packed the gemstone samples and the business cards of the dealers she had met. And, between her folded clothes, she put away the cufflink that had fallen from his shirt.

Then, they returned to their respective lives, restored for another lifetime—just as they used to return from their long walks in the gardens behind the college to go to their respective homes.

"Seeing you was something I had never imagined would happen. Maybe, it was the Almighty's way of reminding me of a time when I was young and believed I could win the world a hundred times over! The evening took me back to times that were so long ago that sometimes, I wonder if they are the product of the imagination of a war-ravaged mind. I do believe that our meeting was a sign. After many initial hiccups, our organisation is now ready to start operations in Bangalore."

Shekhar would be the founder-director of the Indian Military Intelligence Organisation (IMIO), the new hub of India's military intelligence. He would continue the efforts that formed the backbone of the premier institute. She had no doubt that he would continue to rise to the new challenges his mission would bring him.

"I worry about the family, and how they will cope with the extensive travel and busy routine that will continue to be part of my life. As I see Sania grow up, I want her to have the simple upbringing that city life does not offer. Her mother agrees. I feel this is the right time for them to move back to our village. It is, of course, a difficult decision—like yours to enrol Gaurav in boarding school was. But it seems to be what is needed now. Perhaps, this way, I will visit the places of my childhood more often."

Boisterous and easily carried away, Gaurav had been a source of concern. She had seen him boast to the neighbours that he was a maharajah, and his teachers would caution her about his lack of focus. Geetika had worried that he may have inherited Vikram's temperament. She hoped that the strict regimen of a boarding school would help discipline him.

Meanwhile, *Ranima Ki Potli* had become an established brand. Its clientele included celebrities, business families, movie stars, and artistes.

15

"It feels good to be back home after months. Sania has blossomed into a pretty, delicate girl. She is gentle and loving but is strong in her convictions. She wants to change so much in the world, starting from our tiny village! Her mother says that this is the power of belief that being young gives us. I suppose she is right. I too was full of ideas, and as unwavering in my conviction, when I was young. You smile, and I know you will gently remind me that I am like that even now. And as always, you are right.

Don't fret that Gaurav is not as responsible as his elder brother. Don't worry on his account. Your concerns are rooted in the travails of your past and are surely misplaced. You have done an admirable job of raising the two young men. Let them now follow their hearts and build their own lives. You will be surprised—and proud—at how well they do that."

∞

It was time for another change. Gaurav was pursuing his business studies course in Delhi. Gopal was working there too, and both had suggested that she move to Delhi.

It hadn't been an easy decision. The tiny home in the foothills had brought her constancy. The familiar faces, pleasant weather and simple life were close to her heart. The hot climate of the plains couldn't offer her the warmth this place did. However, with her growing clientele, she was travelling more frequently to Delhi. So, she had finally agreed.

Being with her family compensated for the hot weather. Delhi had welcomed her, and she had begun to enjoy the blend of tradition and modernity it offered. She began to explore the theatres, restaurants, and marketplaces that were frequented by businesspeople, artistes, and celebrities, as well as by the middle class.

"I think it is a wonderful idea, Geetu. If a young person is passionate about something, there is no end to what they may achieve. I can understand Gaurav's sentiments, because many years ago, I too was in tearing hurry to fulfil so many ambitions. He is right about banks being forthcoming for loans and business proposals now. While I understand what is holding you back, I have also learned a little bit about being a parent. Do not unwittingly transfer your hesitation and reservations to the young man. If he believes he can make a success of this, let him try. Even if he fails, as I have many times, it will be a lesson he will always remember—and use in all that he decides to do in future."

Economic reforms were underway in India. Gaurav had performed well in his business studies course but had refused the placement offers he had received. He wanted to expand her jewellery business by taking it abroad.

Geetika found herself in a quandary. Vikram's failed business attempts and their consequences weighed on her mind. That was a natural consequence of the troubled times she had seen with Vikram. But there was more that held her back.

Ranima Ki Potli was the only thing that was hers, and hers alone. It had become her passion and her identity. She had been a princess and a wife, roles that life had taken away when she least expected. She had been a mother for more than two decades now. Years of putting her children before her, of worrying about them, of carefully weighing options and selecting only what was best for them. Of bearing the loneliness and the struggle alone. Somewhere along the way, she had become an entrepreneur, a word she had never been familiar with. She had plunged into it with uncertainty but had gradually found her feet—and her confidence. So, she was worried about Gaurav's proposal. What if his confidence was misplaced? At the same time she wondered if she was being selfish about her business. Why was she feeling guilty about being protective of her venture?

"Don't be harsh on yourself. Of course, you feel deeply for your brand. It has given you much more than the money you needed. Perhaps, by letting Gaurav take charge of the company, you will find your burdens lighter. Or is that you do not feel comfortable in lightness anymore?"

Finally, she had overcome her misgivings and allowed Gaurav to join her company and execute his plans.

16

"It was with great difficulty that I could manage a short trip home for Sania's college admission. Yes, Geetu, our college. I was embarrassed when the principal invited me to be the guest of honour at their assembly one day. Hearing my voice boom from the speakers as I addressed the students reminded me of all the assemblies that we were a part of.

Are you wondering if the college has changed? After all, it has been so many years. And nothing in our lives has remained constant. So why would our little college be any different, you wonder. I too was curious, and I decided to explore for myself. Let me tell you about it.

The corridors are still painted dull white and give a perfect backdrop to many a budding romance between new students. The round bench below the peepal tree in the canteen still has enough space for the couple to spend hours together. The samosas they share still taste of each other, more than of the spicy potato filling. The doors of the classrooms are still magical places, where the suitor waits for his lady love. Couples still meet in the red brick building that houses the library, on the pretext of searching for books.

Even now, the semi-circular steps of the amphitheatre reverberate with the mesmerising laughter of the beautiful, young woman. The flower seller continues to park his bicycle outside the gate, so that the young man can buy jasmine strings for his lover's long braid. The stream that runs behind the college wall can still be heard gurgling by the lovers who find each other amidst the trees. The rays of the sun filter through the dense foliage and cast shadows on their faces as they spend the days in endless conversation. The yellow-orange flower petals still fall on their faces, as if showering them with blessings from their personal universe.

As you can see, the visit to the college left me and my memories refreshed.

It is a pleasure to know that Gopal is considering new avenues. Yes, life abroad is different, but nothing that a smart, capable, young man cannot deal with. You are right; he must take the opportunity. And, with the commitment Gaurav is showing, you may soon find yourself without a job! I can imagine how good you must be feeling as a mother. Nothing is more heartwarming for a parent than to realise that their children have created good and fulfilling lives for themselves. Of course, the strength you have infused in them and the love you have showered on them are major contributors to their success!"

The information technology boom had begun. Gopal was moving to America. And *Ranima Ki Potli* was now an international brand. Gaurav had opened an office in Singapore and was building a niche clientele there. He focussed on the operational aspects and left the designing and sourcing of jewels to her. It was a welcome change.

17

"Another new mission, Geetu! Even with my greying hair, a left hand that I have had to relearn how to use, and sight that needs reading glasses, I seem to have a long list of things to do. You must be chuckling and nodding, thinking that I am as restless as I was when I was a young man. I am now back in the offices of the Indian Army. Changing geopolitics makes intelligence as important as hands-on combat, and I will serve as an expert on these matters. This shall hopefully be the end of my nomadic lifestyle, at least for now. Another reminder that new beginnings are everywhere. And that certainly seems to be the case for me, at this point. The circle is the continuum, isn't it?

Children do grow up so fast! Sania's conviction has led her to start a small school for the underprivileged in our village, and her mother is now managing it. Sania, meanwhile, is studying in Pune and continues to dream of changing the world, one step at a time."

Ranima Ki Potli had a new logo. It had been Gautam's idea, as part of his efforts to transform the company. The logo was the imprint of the royal seal, a vestige of her past life. It felt surreal to see it on billboards and magazine advertisements. Gaurav looked after international operations, while she managed the boutique in Delhi. Her bespoke designs in the brocade pouch, and the handwritten scroll that accompanied them, were slices of royalty that customers eagerly looked forward to. India was changing and she was enjoying most of the changes and opportunities it brought her. The buzzing life of Khan Market in Delhi where she had set up her boutique, had become part of her life quickly.

18

"Dear Geetu,

You should have written earlier. I would have liked to meet you. Yes, you are lucky that Delhi offers the best possible medical facilities. I can understand your sentiments, but I can assure you that they are misplaced. For children, especially ones like yours, who have seen their mother go through so much, there is nothing more fulfilling than to be able to care for her. Nothing is more important than to see her healthy and well. And, nothing sadder than to see her in pain and distress. The strain you say you are putting them through is the view of a loving, big-hearted mother. But then, mothers are not always right, are they?

Please assure me that you will take enough rest and follow the doctor's instructions. I know you have gone through life and all its upheavals alone. But that does not mean that it always must be that way. If you need anything, don't hesitate to call your sons, or even your daughter-in-law. The 'troubles' of looking after you, as you put it, will not be heavier than the sorrow they will feel on seeing you suffer.

And, about being alone: you know you are not. You never have been. And never will be."

The niggling pain had become chronic. The cancer had spread by the time the doctors diagnosed it. Gopal and Gaurav had tried to travel to her as frequently as possible. Those long days and longer nights had been difficult, but not more than the initial days of her marriage. At a tender age itself, she had realised that her loneliness was independent of how many people she had around her. Gopal and Gaurav were finally leading the lives they had worked hard for, and she had wanted to give them the least trouble.

The treatment had ended, but life had changed. The weakness lingered. The medicines left her foggy, and pain would recur when she least expected it. It would take her weeks to regain her strength. Once she had felt better, she had taken up Gopal's offer to stay with his family in the USA.

"Of course, you must go! It will be a wonderful experience. And a welcome change, too. I will now be travelling frequently to Europe as a defence expert. The world of internet seems set to change the landscape of military intelligence. It promises to be interesting. Wishing you safe travels and a period of healthy rest and recovery."

Visiting her son's family had brought her much happiness. In Veena, Gopal had found a caring partner who understood his need for being alone and silent often. Geetika cherished the simple joys of being with family. Not having to plan for the weeks and months ahead, and being able to devote herself to her granddaughters, relaxed her. There was much that she had missed in the last several years, but it wasn't too late to reclaim some of those moments and savour them. She hoped Gaurav too would soon find an anchor for the restlessness she could see behind his dynamic leadership of *Ranima Ki Potli*. He seemed content dividing his time between Singapore and Delhi, but she wished he would have someone to share his life and his passion with.

19

"Please don't worry on my account. I am recovering quite well. I know your wishes are always with me. The family has forced a long rest on me, insisting that I recoup my energy.

I still wonder how the doctors found as many blocks in my arteries as they said they did! I have always been physically fit; I could outrun most men half my age. But that night, I woke up feeling my chest being crushed. Anyway, it is yet another reminder of how fragile life is and how little we can prepare for what awaits us.

Today, after many days, I feel strong enough to put pen to paper and write about that day. Everyone told me it was a heart attack. I heard the doctors whisper the term to one another. The nurses murmured the words as they drew blood and poked me with needles. It did make me anxious. But there was another fear in my mind as they wheeled me into the emergency room. Was this how my truth would be revealed? What if they opened me up and found that a tiny part of my heart, somewhere in its core, was missing? That I had been doing military exercises, planning battles, living each day all these years, with a little void in myself? That this void from years ago had been covered and hidden by the events of my life, but had never been filled? And that, even now, it ran deep—beyond my heart and into my soul?

I know that my banter isn't making you smile, and that you will continue to worry until you see me. I don't have to tell you that you are most welcome, any time. I am here, in my government-allotted bungalow in Delhi. Sania's mother returned to the village a few days ago after nursing me for weeks. She has left me in the care of our daughter, who has taken a semester's break from her studies.

My daughter, coming to look after me—such a strange feeling of pride, helplessness, and pride again! I look forward to your meeting this little treasure of my life."

The heart attack had been severe, he had added. It had taken more than two hours for the doctors to remove the clots and bypass some of the blood vessels. Recovery had been slow and tedious.

∞

She had visited him in his colonial-style, government bungalow in the greenest part of the capital, not far from her home.

A sedate-looking young girl had opened the door. Strange as it seemed, she was the spitting image of the little girl in the framed photo on the wall behind her, whose hair was tied in pigtails. Shekhar's beloved mountains provided the perfect backdrop for the photo. The child had blossomed into the beautiful woman standing at the door. Gentle but not shy, Sania welcomed Geetika with a soft, barely audible *Namaste*. Her tall frame and fluid movements, and the charming gleam in her eyes, were Shekhar all over again.

Geetika had stepped into the large hall decorated by dimmed lamps in the corners to find Shekhar standing at the glass door, looking out at the lawn. He was dressed in kurta-pajama and a buttoned-up Nehru jacket. Lean, his posture erect, he had smiled when he had turned around to see her. The familiar glint in his eyes overshadowed the hint of fatigue on his face.

He took in her frame. In his mind, the emerald green of her carefully draped and neatly pinned chiffon saree turned into the pastel that he remembered so well. The shawl draped over her shoulders seemed to flutter like her dupatta had when she had sat behind him on his bicycle. The strands of grey in her shoulder-length hair morphed into the long braid that always left some hair loosely falling around her neck. He could have sworn that the room was redolent of the scent of jasmine flowers that used to adorn her hair her all those years ago.

He steadied himself. Words failed him.

Finally, she spoke. "Let us sit. You look a little tired."

"I am sorry, Geetu! I didn't even ask you to sit. Make yourself comfortable."

As they settled into the upholstered sofa, she took in the mantlepiece lined with his pictures and citations.

Sania, vigilant for her father's comfort, silently propped a cushion behind him before leaving the room.

"This is for you, beta," Geetika called out to her.

The velvet box contained the most beautiful earrings Sania had ever seen. Large, oval, deep-red rubies in the centre, surrounded by a halo of sparkling diamonds; they were breath-taking. Sania hesitated in taking the box from Geetika.

Shekhar stepped in, saying, "Take it, Sania. It is a privilege for you to receive her tastefully designed jewellery. You are blessed."

The young woman had bent down to touch Geetika's feet, only to be stopped midway and embraced by the older woman.

"Let me make tea for you today, Geetu. It will surprise you that I have acquired quite a taste for the delicately flavoured form of the beverage. Though I still love to stop for some *kadak* masala chai by the roadside, whenever I am travelling." He chuckled.

She watched him steady the stump of his left hand. He mixed the single cube of sugar, added the perfect quantity of milk and passed her the cup.

Books lined one entire wall of the room. The dining table seemed more of his work desk, with sheaves of papers and note pads. Another desk had a computer and a telephone. The lawn outside was neat. Overall, the house was simple, yet tastefully furnished. It didn't seem as if he had been living here for long; more like he was a passenger transiting from one station of life to another. Which he was.

She didn't need to spell out these thoughts.

"Geetu, all these years, I have felt at home only while I was immersed in work. The big cities, the little towns, even the foreign lands I visited, never really made me feel at home. It felt as if I was merely passing through them in the journey of life. The only place where I felt I *belonged* is my tiny village, with the mountains holding me in their arms. These houses, hotels, and bungalows hold even less charm now, and I hope to lead a peacefully retired life in my village soon."

She smiled. "Always making plans." He laughed.

This time, she was the one who needed to steady herself.

They talked and talked. They talked of hospitals, doctors, the city that Delhi was transforming into, places that both had visited over the years, their children, and the pride they took in them.

Each soaked in the other's presence, finding solace in silence and their togetherness. They added flashes of memories from this moment to their minds and hearts. The moon crept up silently, its soft yet incandescent light illuminating the lawn. The flames of the fireplace had begun to dance. He watched the glow fall on her face. It felt as if they had always been sitting like this.

It was only when Sania entered the room and removed the clutter of books from the dining table that Geetika realised that hours had passed. Sania silently set the table for two.

"Father has been so excited since morning about your coming. He has been behaving child-like, instructing us to take good care of you and double-checking the arrangements. I can't let you leave without having dinner. Besides, maybe, he will have a better meal today than the one I usually have to coax him to eat."

Shekhar gulped down the medicines Sania brought him, and they moved to the dining table. Sania served them both a generous portion of fragrant dal and warm chapatis.

They ate in silence; the cosy comfortable silence of people who share their daily meals. And life.

"You must be tired."

"No, Geetu. I *was* tired. But now, I feel as if I have never been tired in my life!"

Dinner over, they moved back to the sitting area, this time closer to the fireplace. Geetika waited for Shekhar to settle into his rocking chair and adjusted the footstool so he could stretch his legs. She placed her armchair next to him, close enough for him to smell her lovely, subtle perfume. For a brief, almost non-existent moment, he touched her hand. It felt soft and supple as ever and looked tiny against his large arm. "Your beauty is timeless as ever; untouched by all that you have gone through." He removed his hand and went on. "I was wondering how you would feel meeting an old, frail man like myself."

Softly, she replied with a mischievous twinkle in her eye, "I think I have arrived at the wrong address. I don't see an old man at all. All I see is a youngster who will happily cycle 15 kilometres to look for black wool for someone to knit him a sweater with."

"Aah, you mean the wool that will be used to knit the warmest, softest sweater ever? I have one such, made for me in another lifetime. And whenever I wear it, my bones don't feel the chill anymore. Though I have always wondered if it is the warmth of the wool or the tenderness with which it was woven that has kept me warm all these years."

They spoke of how beautiful spring in Delhi could be, how they still resented its harsh summers—which they had never had to experience in the mountains—and how different today's youth was.

And then, again, they fell into silence.

She watched the moonlight stream in, its shine mixing with the glow of the fireplace. He felt a calmness deep within him. And he knew she did, too.

They spoke about the country, about the border skirmishes and their armed forces.

Then they were silent.

She realised he had fallen asleep. It was time to go home.

She bent down to him, draped her shawl over his outstretched legs and, just for a moment, touched his hand.

And then, she stepped out into the night, taking the soft embers of the fireplace, the shimmering moonlight and their silence with her.

20

"So, yet another change in your life. This time, you are moving farther away. Of course, you are not new to moving houses or to facing different circumstances! For people whose destinies seemed to have been carved in stone, both of us have faced a wide range of circumstances.

You speak of the battle between the heart and the brain. Your heart wonders how you will feel settling down in a faraway land, and if it is right for your son's family. But your brain knows this will be the most appropriate course, given current and future circumstances.

Geetu, you have won so many of these battles, and you have been able to do what was needed without muffling the voice of your heart. And you have done this gracefully—by not pitting the heart and the brain against each other as if in a contest, but by allowing them to join forces. That is how you have emerged the winner. It is something very few people can do.

Even though I call myself a soldier, you have shown so much more courage than me in life. I believe that this decision will be the start of a time when your struggles will finally diminish, and you will find the happiness that you have always deserved—but not had."

Gopal had suggested she move to America. It was a pragmatic solution. Even though the doctors had said she was doing well, she often felt weak. She didn't want her children to be burdened by the thought of her living far away. Gopal had filed for her immigration papers. And she had put up the Delhi house for sale.

"The only place that is important is that which we occupy in our loved one's hearts and they, in ours. I am sure you will agree that our lives are the sum of our lived moments. The memories you

have used to weave this lovely tapestry of your life will accompany you wherever you go. Go, without any unhappiness or doubts, to the life that you will lead with your son and his family."

Living in another continent was something else she had never imagined doing. But then, so many times in her life, the known had turned out to be disturbingly unfamiliar. Whereas, she had easily embraced so much that had been unexpected.

"It is a pleasure to find you adjusting so well to life in California. I hear it has lovely weather. It is also good to know that your health is better and steady. Sometimes, sunshine and people help more than medicines and vitamins!"

Earlier, on her vacations in California, she would feel like a visitor in her son's house. But now, she no longer felt so. Or, a feeling of impermanence. There was a sense of security that she hadn't realised she was missing. This large house, with a basement and an attic, a porch and a small swimming pool, in a country far away, finally felt like home. It felt strange too, that the carefree domesticity she had been bred for was coming to her now, after all these years. And she found solace in it. She had hefted so many burdens in life, that immersing herself in mundane acts like cooking, knitting, and just waiting for everyone to return home in the evening filled her with a pleasant lightness. It gave her a sense of belonging. And not having to plan for the future calmed her.

21

"Geetu,

It is truly an honour to receive one of the highest possible awards in the country. Yet, many times, I wonder if I deserve these accolades. I am just a boy from a small village who wanted to serve his country, and that is what I have tried to do.

These accomplishments I am credited with…have I been the only person responsible for them? Can any achievement be the result of the efforts of a single person? Take me, for example. What would I have been if my life hadn't been touched by so many people? It is said that awards signal the peak of a career. I agree. It is now time to let younger people with new thoughts and ideas take charge.

I have always missed my mountains. These days, I feel the pull of those terraced valleys, the snow-capped peaks and the freshwater streams more than ever. I crave the tranquillity that they have always offered me. My family insists that living alone is not a good idea anymore, and this makes me wonder—am I alone? Have I ever been alone since the year I stepped out of my village to join college?

I can see you nod and hear you tell me to get on without rambling! But, what I say is true. I may have been physically alone at different times of my life, but in my heart and mind, haven't I always had you? And, you do realise that your love is what has given me resilience, don't you? Being loved, and having someone to love, gives us vast and deep reservoirs of strength. Reservoirs that some of us find when we least expect to. It is from these reservoirs that we draw to replenish ourselves when we feel most despondent, as I have, many times in my life.

My current assignments are expected to keep me busy for at least another year. But after that, I plan to finally lead the life of a retired Army veteran.

With Sania now working abroad, my wife finds herself managing our school alone, and I hope to help her. I look forward to teaching young students and motivating them to serve their nation, which is the greatest honour and privilege they can ever hope for."

It had been so much like him to find purpose even in retirement. And to be humble about the Padma award. She had known that he would be happy and cared for in his village, in the surroundings he had grown up in and always carried in his soul. Like she was, here, in California, oceans away from her past.

"Geetu,

It may seem strange to you, but when I was preparing to return to the village, I had very few things to take back with me. Perhaps even fewer than I had left with, when I set out to join the National Defence Academy! My medals and awards, a few books, some photographs and a carton of letters were all that I wanted to carry back home. Here, I have settled into my new routine and am finding peace in it. The occasional invites to appear on television, or for my comments on matters of security, find their way to me. But, I wish to be away from even these things.

You seem to be more excited about Gaurav's falling in love than he himself might be! I understand that the suspense has intrigued you. Give him some time. Soon, he will share with you who it is that has captured his spirited heart."

Geetika lingered on this letter for a while, running her hands over the sheet of paper. Then, she carefully folded it and put it back in the Airmail envelope with red and blue stripes along its edges. This was the last letter in the pile; she had received it a few months ago. The box was empty now; she had carefully stacked all the letters on the table.

The tears came as a flood. Strangely, they dissolved the lump in her throat. She was grateful to her heart for finally allowing her to cry. She had been scared that the lump would stay in her throat forever, staunchly blocking her airway and eventually, obstructing it and suffocating her to death. She cried.

She caressed the box, as if another letter would appear magically. When it didn't, she hugged the box close to her chest and let her tears flow. It was late afternoon. Everyone would start returning soon: Veena and Tara, followed by Uma and finally, Gopal.

Till then, she could cry, be alone with the letters spread out around her, hold the envelopes and feel Shekhar's presence in them.

Sometime later, she reached for the bundle of letters. One by one, she began returning them to the plastic box, exactly as they had been arranged earlier.

Then, she got up to put the box back in the bottom of the wardrobe. This time, her knees were steady, and her legs felt strong. Just as they used to, when Shekhar and she used to walk deep into the countryside, along the meandering stream. Hand in hand, they would reach the point where the gurgling stream entered the placid river and climb over the large boulders with rounded edges. At the riverbank, she would perch herself on one of the boulders, hitch her saree up and let the water wash over her feet. They would sit there for hours, feeling the tiny pebbles on the riverbed with their feet and love in their hearts. They would reach for a few pebbles and fling them into the river, competing to see who could throw them farther. Bickering about whose ripples had lasted longer, they would end up falling into each other's arms, laughing. And at twilight, they would walk back, the blaze of the setting sun warming their souls and its reflection shimmering in the water behind them.

22

She heard Veena's car in the driveway. The sound of Tara reciting a kindergarten rhyme filled the corridor. The little girl stopped by at her grandmother's room before going upstairs, eager to share details of her day. "Grandma…you know, we learned a new poem today! It is about a train engine!" Tara climbed up on the poster bed and recited the poem for her grandma.

"Lovely," Geetika replied.

Tara sensed, as children often can, that the mood in her grandmother's room was different today; more sombre. She cuddled with Geetika. As Geetika caressed her forehead, Tara saw the newspaper, still open on Page 3.

Tara pointed to the picture of Shekhar, the one showing him receiving the Padma award.

"Who is this, Grandma?"

"Someone I used to know a long time ago."

"When you were in India?"

"Yes, my dear."

"Is he a prince?"

"Yes. He was a prince. Like none other."

"Grandma, Papa is calling you to the study! There are emails he wants you to see."

Must be some designs for Ranima Ki Potli, she thought. Designs came for her approval from the studio. "Uma, tell him I am tired. I would like to rest."

Probably hearing her words, Gopal called out, "Ma, come here for a moment. Gaurav has sent us an important mail."

She walked into the study.

"Ma, Gaurav has sent us a picture. Finally, we get to meet his fiancée, even if only through a photo."

The girls were standing around the table, discussing the Indian clothes they would wear for the wedding. They had grown even more excited after seeing the photo in the email.

"Grandma, our new aunt is simply gorgeous!"

Curious, Geetika sat in the chair in front of Gopal's laptop. Gopal enlarged the photo a bit, so that she could see it clearly. Her breath caught. It was a face she had seen once before—in a bungalow in Delhi. And the gleam in the eyes was something she had seen every day for a lifetime. The beautiful eyes gazing at her from the screen had honesty, warmth and kindness, qualities she had seen in another set of eyes. A pure, deep-red ruby sparkled on each of the young woman's ears.

Sania.

And yet again, Geetika's eyes welled up. But these were tears of joy. And of some other, inexplicable, emotion. Instinctively, a soft sigh escaped her lips and she smiled through her tears. Her Shekhar would continue to be a part of her life.

∞

Humsafar

Humsafar – Companion

Love is the bridge between you and everything.

—Rumi

1

Present Day

"Did you see this?" Rajat asked Rachna as he placed the newspaper, strategically folded at a half-page advertisement, next to her bowl of fruit on the breakfast table.

Rachna was taken aback.

Rajat continued talking. "This picture…isn't this the doctor whose books you have in the study?"

The colour drained from Rachna's face. Rajat noted that she hadn't even picked up the newspaper.

"Check it out, Rachna. This is a new hospital being inaugurated today. Looks interesting to me. Do you know anything about it?"

"No…"

She regained her composure, but studiously ignored the newspaper.

He persisted.

"Rachna, why are you so disinterested? This is an exciting new concept, which we could explore for our hospital, too."

Rachna silently added the stevia into Rajat's tea and passed him the cup.

She didn't need to look at the advertisement to know that Rajat was speaking about Venkat.

"In fact, maybe you could attend the inauguration today?" Rajat said.

She almost dropped the pitcher of milk she was giving Sanvi for her cereal.

"Careful, Mom!"

"Is everything okay, Rachna?

"Yes, yes," she was quick to reply.

"Papa, it's time for the school bus," Sanvi piped up.

"Do you want a ride to the metro station?" Rajat turned to Pranav as he asked this question.

Pranav quickly washed down his sandwich with a cold coffee. Phone in one hand, he reached for his backpack. It was his first month at medical college. The euphoria of his admission to the college was yet to give in to the academic pressure. It was unlike Rachna to remind him how unhealthy it was to gulp down his food, or to ignore Sanvi's reminder to buy her the acne ointment. But this morning, she did both.

2

Breakfast in their cosy bungalow in Delhi always put Rachna in high spirits. It was a routine she had started when the children had been in primary school. And even now, with Sanvi having graduated from enjoying unicorns to being a teenager obsessed with Rock music, and Pranav in college, it remained a part of their lives. A thumbs-up to Rajat for an important meeting, a best-of-luck hug for Sanvi's test or a gentle reminder to Pranav for a haircut—everything found place at the breakfast table and filled her heart with warmth.

But, not today.

She finally looked at the newspaper. Rajat had not been mistaken. The picture was indeed of Venkat. The five hard-bound volumes of *Approach to Paediatric Medicine* authored by him were essential reading for thousands of medical students and doctors all over the country.

She was aware of the new children's hospital built on a public-private partnership model. It was a network of digitally connected healthcare facilities. The network had nodal clinics in most big cities of India. Satellite centres in villages and towns across the country would be connected to these. And regional care facilities across the country would support this pyramidal structure. The apex centre in Gurgaon, on the outskirts of Delhi, was a state-of-the-art hospital. Telemedicine consultations and online consultation referrals blended technology with healthcare. Making medical care available to children in the remote interiors of the country had been Venkat's dream for as long as she could remember.

Half an hour later, when Rajat returned, Rachna had still not finished her breakfast. She was still at the table, lost in her thoughts.

"What's the matter? You haven't eaten anything. Don't you have any appointments today?" Rajat asked her.

"I do. Just wasn't feeling hungry."

"I will be leaving early today. Some production line issues."

"Sure." She nodded absently.

He went upstairs to get dressed for work.

It was unusual for her to not ask about an issue at the factory. The mention of 'Paalna', their charitable hospital, hadn't perked her up, either. These inconsistencies played on his mind.

When he returned downstairs, the newspaper was right where he had left it; folded at the same place. The flower delivery service he had subscribed to for Rachna had sent carnations. They sat on the console table by the door, waiting to be put in water.

"I'd better get going. I have a busy day," said Rajat as he walked out of the house.

The door clicked shut behind him.

3

Rachna looked out into the garden. The wind chimes were tinkling and the roses were in full bloom. Butterflies, welcome visitors in the spring, flitted amidst the potted plants. The bright pink and creamish-white bracts of the carefully pruned bougainvillea bushes draped the boundary wall. The daisies had flowered well. The lilies would follow, in their magical April rhythm.

It was a lovely morning, perfect for some coffee before she left for work. But the disturbing vibes of the black-and-white newsprint outweighed the allure of her colourful garden. And the coffee wasn't strong enough to refresh her thoughts. She finally looked at the page at which the paper had been lying open since earlier that morning.

The photograph was a grainy, old, black-and-white one that looked even older in its thumbnail size. The white coat and stethoscope around his neck conjured up the typical image of an experienced doctor. It was the same photo that graced the back cover of all his books. Through the picture and his books, many doctors would feel a vague sense of familiarity with a person they had never seen or met. But they only knew of Venkat, the expert in paediatric medicine. Rachna, on the other hand, was one of the very few people who knew Venkat the person. It was another matter that this was Venkat's and her secret. And it would always remain so. The burden of this knowledge had been weighing her down for the last few days—ever since the postman had delivered the Speed Post package a few days ago. The cloth-lined envelope had her name and address handwritten on it.

"Dear Rachna,

I hope you are well.

I am enclosing an invitation for the inauguration of the hospital—the inauguration I have been working towards, all these years. It is a part of the public-private partnership scheme of the Ministry of Health. Using telemedicine and remote consultation, we can now hope to provide healthcare to the sickest children even in the remote interiors of the country. It is also a good opportunity for charitable hospitals like yours to associate with this model. I am sending you the application form.

This hospital is the only dream I have had the courage to dream in my life. And there is no greater joy than seeing it fulfilled.

Venkat."

There was a white envelope that carried her full name: Rachna Arora, Director, Sunshine Children's Centre, Delhi. It contained an ivory-white invitation card with black embossed print, stamped VIP. She could imagine Venkat, his face intent with concentration, writing this letter in his neat, slanting handwriting. The light of the table lamp would be focused on the uncluttered desk as he wrote, pausing now and then to take a sip from a steel tumbler of filter coffee.

The sight of the yellow, cloth-lined envelope opened a floodgate of memories. Memories of case records being filled, progress sheets being written late into the night, small needles being injected into the delicate veins of tiny babies, the cacophony of sounds of the Emergency ward. Since the day the letter arrived, these thoughts and memories of working with Venkat had crept up on her. She had pushed them away.

But she couldn't brush away the fact that it wasn't Venkat's envelope that was troubling her; it was Rajat's behaviour. His actions had been perplexing. And not just today. For the past few days, he had been watchful of her in a strange way. Last week, he had suddenly quizzed her about telemedicine. Then, the other day, she had seen

Venkat's textbooks rearranged on the bookshelves. Could Rajat possibly suspect the truth? Why else would he have brought up Hyderabad in a conversation, on the pretext of having a new client there? The thought made her want to retch. Rajat, who could be shy and withdrawn, could also be easily enraged. Everyone knew the almost-Jekyll-and-Hyde transformation that could come over him. There was no one who hadn't been at the receiving end of his temper. Except for the children. With them, he had always been so soft, tender, and forgiving. He had mellowed significantly over time, though, especially in the last few years.

And today, he had probed her after seeing the newspaper. Despite her reluctance to discuss the advertisement, he had persisted. The tension had been palpable, and she had been relieved when he left home early.

4

The carnations today were a perfect white, her favourite flower and colour. The subscription to the delivery service had been Rajat's gift to her after they had visited a flower show recently. Rachna loved plants and nurtured her garden with as much love and tenderness as she nurtured her family and hospital.

Her phone buzzed as she was arranging the flowers in the vase. A text message. From her mother-in-law.

Thank you for the oil of wintergreen.

A smiley was affixed after the sentence. Rachna was nonplussed. The bottle of oil she had ordered for Rajat's mother had been in his car. Hadn't he told her he needed to go to the office early? But it looked like he had actually gone to meet his mother. Why had he lied to her? Another instance of him acting strangely.

Something was definitely amiss. The charged atmosphere at home was a throwback to those turbulent days immediately after their wedding—and Mohit's wedding, too. Mohit, Rajat's younger brother, had got married a few days after them and had joined Rajat's firm. It should have been a time of joy for the entire family. But things had gone horribly wrong. Those were days she did not want to revisit. Ever.

She shuddered. Of course, over the years, so much had eclipsed the memories of those troubled times. A lot of water had passed under the bridge since then. But there was no getting away from the fact that the turbulence continued to affect all of them deeply from time to time.

Suddenly, as her thoughts went back to those days, Rachna felt drained.

But her recollection of old memories continued inexorably, rushing at her like an oncoming train. She recalled that Rajat had been tense and irritable even before they had left for their honeymoon. Once they reached Mauritius, however, he had allowed the pressures of work to dissolve. They had revelled in the beauty of the beaches, and in their togetherness. After returning to India, he had been very busy at work again. It was then that the waves of anger that could consume him despite his otherwise soft-spoken nature had become evident to her. Teething troubles of a new business venture, she had assumed. And then, after Mohit's sudden death, everything had changed for the worse.

It had taken years for all of them to come to terms with that tragedy. But again, in the last few days, she had felt an uneasiness that reminded her of the unfortunate turn life had taken years ago. Was it about to take another nasty turn now?

The sun was getting brighter. It would be a warm day, a prelude to the harsh summer of Delhi. Getting up to close the sheer curtains, Rachna felt a sudden bout of dizziness. She decided to cancel her appointments and stay home. She hoped that would drive the fatigue away.

5

The sun's rays fell on the wall of the living room. Painted deep ochre, this was a part of the house everyone in her family cherished. The eclectic collection of photo frames in different colours and designs chronicled their journey as a family. The first picture was more than two decades old, but the beauty of Auli and the slippery trek were vivid memories. Rajat was holding her gently at the waist from behind. Her sunglasses were reflecting the bright sunshine. That was where she had fallen in love with the mountains. The hill stations near Bombay seemed to aspire to these Himalayan heights—and fall short in comparison.

Then there was the picture of Pranav's first birthday, with all the little children crowded around the birthday cake; a day more special for the parents than for the birthday boy. Rajat had come home with a tiny box decorated with ribbons.

"What is this? We must not pamper him like this. Besides, Rajat, small objects aren't safe with little kids. You know that!"

"Yes, doctor mom. I know that, even if I am not a busy doctor who looks after children all day. Calm down and listen. This is for you."

It was a white gold chain and a sparkling diamond pendant.

"It's beautiful, Rajat! But, it isn't my birthday."

"It doesn't have to be. It's for being in my life; being the most amazing person, wife, mother."

Spa vouchers for her, cancelling his golf sessions to help her with the renovation of the clinic, getting his parents to babysit while they checked out the latest restaurants...he would surprise her often.

There were pictures of Pranav playing with toy trains, Lego blocks and electricity kits as he grew up. Rajat would patiently do various activities with him. Even when Pranav had gone to sleep, Rajat would spend hours making the models.

"Come, let's put this train together."

"Rajat, you are behaving like a child. How will I manage three children in the house?" The news of her second pregnancy had brought him a joy he had never believed possible. But the pregnancy hadn't been easy on her. Nor had Rajat, for that matter. Overprotective, almost overbearing, he would check on her many times a day.

"I will send the driver from the factory. Don't want you taking extra stress."

The driver would arrive with her favourite chocolate milkshake or the bhelpuri she had developed a craving for.

"Rajat, I will become quite lazy at this rate!"

"You are always so busy with your patients. You need to look after yourself."

The delight and fulfilment Sanvi had brought them were reflected in many of the other photos hung on the wall.

The one of Pranav watching a new-born Sanvi sleep with a mix of curiosity and wonder. That of Sanvi in her grandmother's lap during her *mundan* ceremony. Rajat had nagged the barber to death. "Be careful, don't hurt her!" He had insisted on selecting a deep pink silk saree for Rachna to wear on the occasion. It remained one of her favourite sarees. And then, one of her favourite pictures, in which Rajat was hugging the children.

Another photo showed Pranav on his first day of school. Hair slickly combed and wearing the school uniform, belt and shiny shoes. She remembered what a difficult day it had been. Not on account of Pranav—he had been happy with the idea of playing with toys and reading new books—but because of Rajat, who had driven her up the wall with his concerns!

"Are you sure he is not too young? We didn't start school until we were five!"

"What if other kids bully him? He is so shy."

"Have you told the teachers that he may need help with his water bottle?"

"Are you sure he will be comfortable?"

Then there were pictures of their holidays. They would drive off to Mussoorie, Nainital, Shimla, Manali. She loved the mountain breeze and the misty clouds that would drift towards them. The children would recite their favourite rhymes and sing along with the latest blockbusters as she passed them sandwiches and Frooti in tetra packs.

In the winters, they would escape to Bombay. Partying with friends, catching up with her parents, and the children having fun with their cousins, they would ring in the new year. There was even a picture from a Christmas party, with Rajat dressed as Santa.

Friendships from college had endured, and the long-time friends met often. Their love and understanding would often come up in the many parties they hosted or attended.

A photo near a corner of the wall showed Rachna and Rajat hugging each other after winning the 'Most Charming Couple' title at a party.

"So, tell us, how did you two find each other?" a friend had asked them that day.

"We were destined to meet each other in Matheran. I had gone there for a vacation. And she was right there, waiting for me in the lobby of the resort!" Rajat's reply had made her smile. How romantic he made their chance meeting seem!

The picture of her at the ice cream parlour, chocolate sauce smudged on her cheek, made her smile impishly to herself.

"Didi, do you and Jiju ever fight? It doesn't seem like it!"

"Of course, we fight. We fight like cats and dogs, like two children over a toy—and even like two sparring warriors!"

"Then how do you patch up?"

"Once we are done fighting, we allow ourselves to cool off. Then one of us suggests we go out for ice cream."

"Ice cream?"

"Yes, that's something we have always enjoyed. So, we go out for ice cream. And we order only one. Either Rajat's favourite flavour, which is usually something fruity—like strawberry or mango or black currant—or mine, which is chocolate or coffee. We share the cold delight. Then we order a favourite flavour of the other person and share that too," Rachna remembered explaining. "Like the ice cream flavours, we are different in some ways, but we can share our differences and taste the sweetness of life together."

"Didi, you and Jiju are amazing. Such a perfect relationship!"

"No dear, a relationship we started working on many years ago, and have never stopped working on."

There were photographs of her hospitals, Sunshine and Paalna. She had worked passionately for both, but she wouldn't have been able to handle them without Rajat. She would happily attend to the patients, train other doctors, and ensure the medicine supplies. But for managing the hospitals, she would always turn to him. He handled the administration and accounts exactly as he did for his factory—meticulously and efficiently.

The pictures of the children's school events and prize distribution ceremonies showed their changing interests and growing-up years. At Pranav's school farewell, he had chosen to wear the tie Rajat had worn for their engagement. The two most important men in her life were standing together in the photo, but not shoulder-to-shoulder. The resemblance between them was striking, except that Pranav was five inches taller than Rajat.

Always proud of her professional achievements, Rajat had insisted that she put up the pictures of her giving academic talks and presentations. He had selected one in which she was being felicitated by the Association of Paediatric Medicine. The most recent picture on the wall was from their twenty-fifth wedding anniversary celebrations. The children had arranged a lovely surprise party, with games, champagne, cake, and sumptuous food.

This photo wall was the highlight of their home. It never failed to cheer her up. But today, the anxiety continued to bubble within her. The agitation that had built up in the last few days had peaked today. What was going on in her husband's brilliant mind was a mystery. Could he possibly suspect the truth? Where would all this take them? Her lovely family. *Their* lovely life. It all felt so fragile. Was it a heartbeat away from shattering into a hundred pieces?

6

Rajat had closed the door behind him and realised he had forgotten his blood pressure medicines. Deciding against going back in to get them, he got into the car instead. In any case, he was sure they wouldn't have helped calm the agitation he was feeling.

At the breakfast table, he had deliberately passed Rachna the newspaper folded on that page. Her reaction had been strange and had added to the unrest in his already disturbed mind.

It had all started a few days ago, when Rachna had called him at work.

"Can you pick up Sanvi after her extra class? I have a number of appointments."

"Sure. What time do I need to reach school?"

"4:30 pm."

"Ok."

On the way from his office to school, he had stopped by at home to pick up the ID card issued by Sanvi's school to the guardians of children. A guardian could pick up their ward from the school only by showing this card. Rummaging through the drawers in the desk, Rajat had seen the package with a Speed Post sticker on it.

It was unusual to see Rachna's name without the honorific 'Dr'. The prefix had become a part of her name. Curious, he had opened the package to find an envelope containing an ivory-white card with golden edges and the emblem of the Indian government embossed on it. It was an invite for the inauguration of a hospital.

Running late, Rajat had placed it back in the drawer and rushed to pick Sanvi up.

But the next evening, he had returned to the desk. And, the envelope. It was unusual of Rachna to not have mentioned the invite to him.

He had carefully taken the envelope out of the drawer. Cloth-lined, it had a handwritten return address. The sender's name, Venkat R, seemed both unfamiliar and familiar. There was a letter and a folded form that Rachna had begun filling out. He read the letter and opened the invitation card again. It was an event that would surely be of interest to Rachna.

He began to sift through the other contents of the drawer. Most of them seemed to have been undisturbed for a long time. A few old income tax documents, an old report card from Sanvi's primary school, a Mother's Day card made by Sanvi and Pranav when they had been little. And then, another envelope with the logo of a playschool; Pranav's or Sanvi's, he wasn't sure. He wasn't surprised. Rachna had the children's growing-up memorabilia tucked away everywhere. He opened this envelope, expecting to find a note or a doodle from the children.

Instead, he found a photograph. A single photograph. It was old, but not very worn; slightly faded, but not eared out and frayed. It showed Rachna standing at a pani puri stall, trying to keep her hair in place with one hand. In her other hand, she was holding the ubiquitous paper plate with the street side snack. The man with her was signalling to the vendor, perhaps asking him to hand him the next pani puri ball. Neither Rachna nor the man was facing the camera, and the vendor occupied almost half of the frame. Rajat couldn't figure out where the picture had been taken or recognise the man in the picture.

Then, suddenly, the name on the envelope, the picture, and the photograph he had seen on many textbooks in their house—all came together with a click. He had seen the face on the books lining the shelves in the study. He remembered that the name was written on the cover of each of those books.

Venkat. And the handwriting on the cloth-lined yellow envelope matched that of the short autographs written on each of those books. Autographs addressed to Rachna.

Venkat. One of her many teachers and mentors during her training days. Must be from her time in Bombay, he thought.

He had remained distracted at work the whole day. The envelope and the photograph had lingered in his mind, and he couldn't shake off the doubts that were forming there. Yet, he wasn't able to ask Rachna about them, either. He didn't know why.

Feeling the beginning of a headache, he had picked up the phone.

"Hi! How's work?"

He could hear a baby wailing in the background. "Really busy," came Rachna's reply.

As he had expected.

"All well, Rajat?" she asked when he drew out his silence a bit.

He had rushed through breakfast and had been restless last night, too.

But he said, "Yes, just finished a meeting and was wondering if I can take you out for ice cream."

She laughed. Ice cream was their thing. Everyone knew that her idea of a treat was to head out to Nirula's ice cream parlour for one of their special flavours. She was their kids' friends' favourite paediatrician because she never said no to ice cream.

"You know I'd love to come, but I have a lot of patients." So she would be busy for a while.

He had returned home to the drawer where the envelope had been hidden away. Hidden away? Yes, of course. She hadn't told him about it. Not even when he had specifically asked her, "So, anything new? Any ideas related to Paalna? We could think of expanding it."

He had told himself he was overreacting. Yet, he reached for the drawer's handle again.

He hadn't bothered with the other papers. It was the photograph he had wanted to see. He was sure the person with her was Venkat. Rachna's expression in the photo was one of simple, uncomplicated happiness. The kind we experience before our lives are burdened with pressures and responsibilities.

But then, Venkat and Rachna could have been together in the photo for any number of natural reasons. Venkat had been Rachna's teacher. This picture could have been taken when she was in college, or during her training years. Medical students and young doctors rarely got time off for fun. This may have been one of those rare moments when a group of them had rushed out for a quick snack. A group, because someone else had clicked the picture; they obviously hadn't posed for it. So, no big deal about the picture. Then why was he unable to stop analysing it?

But Rachna had so many other photos with her friends, teachers, colleagues, and even her juniors. Why then had she kept this photograph separately? Why did he keep coming back to this one?

The constant stress was making him feel weary.

He took out all the papers again; read through the letter once more. There was a slender ring binder file with handwritten notes in the drawer, that he hadn't noted the other day. Most of the notes were in Rachna's handwriting. And some, he now realised, were in Venkat's. They were filled with medical information: names, classifications, and algorithms that doctors use to exercise some feeling of control over the maladies of the human body. Was there an algorithm that would help him work through this muddle of questions now?

So what if Rachna had been colleagues or even friends with Venkat? Or with anyone else. What had made him assume that the people in the picture had been more than friends?

And even if they had been, so what? Even if she had been in a relationship with someone back then, how did it matter now? He was mature enough to accept and understand that.

He needed to stop overthinking. He began rearranging the contents of the drawer. While putting the photograph back into its envelope, he noticed something he hadn't, so far. He had seen her hand on her forehead, and her hair askew in what must have been a breeze. What he hadn't noticed was the band on her finger; gleaming as its diamond picked up a ray of sunshine. It was the ring he had slipped onto her finger at their engagement ceremony. Also, he saw the silhouette of a white statue in the background. The Buddha statue in Hussain Sagar Lake. In Hyderabad. Where Rachna had trained in neonatology after their marriage.

Over the next few days, he hadn't been able to get this entire episode out of his mind. His routine alternated between pretending to be busy with work and being extra attentive to Rachna's responses. He had obsessively searched for Venkat's details on the internet. The website of the hospital where he worked highlighted his distinguished career. Search results showed the numerous academic and research papers he had authored. He seemed to be a brilliant physician and a distinguished academician. But there was nothing about his personal life.

Rajat was sure Venkat had worked with Rachna in Bombay, before their marriage, as well as in Hyderabad, soon after it. It was a turmoil he had been unable to resolve. He had upped his gym routine, hoping that the intensity of the workouts would eclipse that of his feelings. Why had Rachna kept his letter a secret? What else was she hiding? This morning, she had been startled when he had shown her the ad. That, the breakfast table discussion and his comments should have been enough to make her show him Venkat's invitation. But she had chosen not to do so.

Which is why his suspicion had deepened.

7

Rachna would notice that the car was still in the driveway if he sat there any longer. So he had decided to visit his mother. Rachna had ordered some wintergreen oil for his mother's joint pain a few days ago. He would drop it off.

After Mohit's death, his parents had never found the courage to return to the house they had so lovingly built. They had opted for this smaller home, instead. The gate of the house, in need of a greasing, creaked as he opened it. Noting that a cast iron lamp bracket was hanging loose, he made a mental note to remind Rachna to call the electrician.

His mother opened the door and motioned him to be silent. He had interrupted her morning pooja ritual. He waited for her to complete it. She placed fresh flowers in front of the photos of Mohit and his father that she had placed in a corner of the living room and folded her hands in prayer.

After his father passed away last year, Rachna had tried to get his mother to move in with them. But she said she preferred to live here. The two most important women in his life shared a great relationship. Rachna relied heavily on her mother-in-law's advice and appreciated the yummy delicacies she made for her grandchildren. Both women enjoyed their lunch-and-shopping sessions.

Rajat watched his mother, silent and reflective, and waited for her to mark his forehead with the vermilion paste. Of course, she had never recovered fully from Mohit's death; how could you expect her to? Those had been such troubled times for everyone. It should have been a new, joyous phase for the entire family; one that set the stage for their future. It *had* set the stage for their future, albeit in the most unexpected ways.

Seeing him lost in thought, his mother gently asked him, "Is everything ok?"

"Yes, Ma. Just wanted to give you this. And have a cup of your special ginger tea."

He could feel the headache beginning to overwhelm him.

The geraniums and petunias in the hanging planter pots with their woven rope baskets had flowered well. Rachna had managed to get his mother interested in gardening, too. Feeling a sudden urge to distract himself, he got up.

"Ma, where is the tool kit? Let me fix the bulb outside."

"Don't you have to go to office?"

"No, a meeting got cancelled."

The monotony of hammering the bulb holder back in place helped him calm down.

A photo of Rachna with Venkat didn't mean they had had an affair. But it was obvious that Rachna had kept Venkat's letter and invite a secret. She had even begun filling in the application form he had sent for Paalna. And she had not mentioned that, either. There had to be more than what met the eye. It was not just the suspicion that Rachna and Venkat had been in a relationship that was bothering him. He had been thinking of Mohit, too. It was strange how many of the memories from the days after Mohit's death had crept up on him often in the last few days. Things were different now, he told himself. Those days were gone forever. Yet, he was sometimes unable to get a grip on himself, however hard he tried.

The commotion in his head was back; the meandering thoughts and memories had stopped again at what was the family's bedrock: Rachna. Rachna was the glue that held their lives together. Everything would come apart when she travelled for her conferences. Despite the many written notes and reminders from her, Rajat would struggle to remember instructions for the staff and the details of their kids' timetable, activities, food and exams. And the kids would gleefully gobble up takeaways. The cogs seemed to stop turning until she returned and picked up things from where she had left them.

When his friends asked him the secret of his successful marriage, Rajat would laugh the question off. But today, he wondered if the laugh was on him. Was their perfect marriage based on a lie?

Where did they go from here? Why was he unable to stop suspecting the most important relationship and person in his life?

He knew what he needed to do. He would go and ask her. He needed to know the truth.

8

"Good morning, sir."

He nodded and went past the assistant. The clinic, which was usually filled with the chatter of anxious parents and wailing babies, was silent today. The lights were off, the blinds drawn. The examination chamber was empty.

"Sir, ma'am isn't here. She called in the morning to cancel her appointments."

"Yes, I know. I came to pick up some papers she left here yesterday." He was flustered and embarrassed. And angry.

"Of course, sir. I will send you some coffee."

More secrets. She hadn't turned up at the clinic. If she had meant to take the day off, why didn't she tell him in the morning? The inauguration of Venkat's hospital was scheduled for today. Did she plan to attend it? Or did she plan to meet Venkat before the event? Maybe they had continued their association and been in touch over the years. The thought seemed so unlikely, given how involved Rachna and Rajat were in each other's lives, but there seemed to be no other explanation for her odd behaviour. None of what was happening seemed to be real, anyway.

He pulled apart the giraffe-patterned curtains. Daylight filled the room. The room was warm and cosy, designed to make anxious children and their parents comfortable. Sanvi had selected the animal theme for the room, and the blue step-up stool and wooden steps for the examination couch matched the colour of the hippos on the wall. Rajat sat at Rachna's table and took in the animal-shaped pen stands and medicine dispensers.

Her diplomas and degrees hung on the wall; framed and neatly arranged, they were a testimony to her hard work and training. A separate corner was devoted to the charts and graphs she used to monitor the growth and development of her patients so diligently.

Who was the real Rachna, he wondered? The brilliant doctor who cared deeply for her patients, or the one who kept secrets from him? Mementoes and certificates from academic events and scientific sessions were a proud testimony to her achievements. But did his wife have another conquest under her belt, a conquest she hadn't told him about? He could feel his stomach churning. The photograph in her drawer, with the shining diamond on her fingers and the happiness in her smile as she stood with Venkat, was as real as could be. In stark contrast, her reaction today had been of discomfort and avoidance. And, on top of that, she had not told him she was taking the day off. There could be no doubt that she was hiding Venkat's letter from him. He should have connected the dots much earlier. Instead, he had ignored the red flags. And now, here he was, alone in her clinic, expecting answers from her! Where *was* Rachna? Maybe she had other plans? Venkat was in Delhi for the inauguration, after all. Did she have a VIP pass to the event—another secret?

"Thanks for the coffee," he told the assistant and walked out of the clinic a little later.

He was left with no choice but to confront his wife. She would have to come clean. He would go home and wait for her to return from wherever she had gone. After lying to him.

9

1992

Rachna had always wanted to become a doctor. In the wards of the unkept but efficient government hospital, she found the words of the books and teachers come alive. A surgeon wielding sophisticated equipment to remove the source of trouble. A physician fitting together clues to solve a mystery. An ophthalmologist giving people new windows to the world. She would imagine a career in each specialty of medicine. She enjoyed looking after pregnant women and ensuring healthy childbirth. Getting a peek into the human body as a radiologist or pathologist held her attention, as did the fast-paced life of an emergency physician. But all that was waylaid when she had her first spell of duty in the paediatric ward.

The paediatric ward of the sprawling hospital touched her as nothing else had. She was transfixed. She had never imagined how powerful the grip of a tiny human being could feel on her finger. It was overwhelming to realise the responsibility parents placed in a paediatrician or paediatric surgeon. The paediatric ward was also where she met Venkat for the first time. The routine of a new resident doctor could be considered punishing by many, but he didn't mind it. Studying to be a children's doctor was his calling. His bedside manner and his approach with the most vulnerable of the babies gave her so much to learn from.

Having seen sickness in children at close quarters, Venkat had vowed to do all he could to prevent it. The joy of being able to heal children and the inspiration she drew from Venkat made her settle on paediatrics as a career. Training to be a paediatrician was an arduous task, with rigorous duty schedules and gruelling night shifts. But it was also an exciting and satisfying time. For her, and for thousands of other young, freshly minted doctors across the country, this was the norm. They would trade in family occasions for emergency duties; work for hours without rest and go without sleep for days. Short breaks with tiny cups of tea would be enough to refresh them for many hours. Duty hours would end, but they would remain in the hospital, finishing pending work and discussing cases. On rare days off, they would go home and enjoy some much-cherished sleep and home-cooked food.

Vacations and getaways were rare, but they were a welcome respite to her busy routine. The long weekend in Matheran with her parents had been one of those occasions when she could get away from the ever-buzzing pager. The cool breeze and misty weather of the Sahyadri Hills had soothed her frayed nerves.

"Rachna, tell us if you are seeing someone. It will be safe to assume that, if you are in a relationship, it will be with someone at work. You don't seem to have much of a life other than that, these days," her father told her on their first day in Matheran.

She laughed. "Papa, hospital wards are hardly the most romantic of places."

But they were, for so many of her friends who were finding partners there and falling in love.

And then there was Venkat. In the last two years, he had become a constant presence in her life. The wards, library, clinics and the many shifts of duty; he was always around. He would sit for hours in the library reading, while she worked on her presentations. He would make an extra effort to show her the subtle signs of an unusual disease in the wards or help her with the long tables and charts that were part of her dissertation. A shared passion for paediatrics drew them close. The busy schedules ensured that they spent most of their time together.

Rachna's sensitivity and obvious affection for him made her one of the few people with whom Venkat shared little parts of himself. As they worked together, his accounts of diseases in children, medicines and vaccines began to be interspersed with vignettes from his life. His rural background and the stories of being orphaned early in life and being cared for by distant relatives touched Rachna. She would listen sympathetically and try to imagine how all those experiences would have affected him. They had grown close.

The teacher and the taught; the mentor and the mentee—these descriptions were inadequate for them. He had always been a reticent and withdrawn person. The occasional relationship he had been in had been short-lived. But this was different. When they worked together, he felt a kinship he had never expected to feel with anyone. He couldn't understand the emotions she stirred in him, and would push them into the recesses of his mind. Then, he would steal a glance at her in the library or in the crowded clinic, and the feelings would return. He wouldn't allow his gaze to linger, but the feelings would engulf him. He had not realised when the tenderness he felt for her transformed into love. A love that deepened each day. The stronger his feelings became, the more reticent he was. He could never summon the courage to tell her that he had fallen in love with her.

The ward rounds, the clinics they attended together, the scores of children they worked with over those years and the busy shifts in the emergency rooms—all this added up to a very fulfilling training period for Rachna. She was aware of his presence in her life, and she valued it. In him, she was grateful to have found a mentor who was also a friend.

Rachna had laughed off the discussion with her father and snuggled up in the blanket with her Walkman.

Later that evening, she had been enjoying the sunset from the large sit-out in the lobby of the resort.

"Hi!! I am Rajat! Can you suggest a good trekking route somewhere here?"

If it hadn't been for Mohit who had encouraged him to strike a conversation with Rachna, he wouldn't have mustered the courage to do so. It had taken Mohit 15 minutes of coaxing to make him overcome his shyness. In spite of being a good student and an active debater in school and college, Rajat remained diffident in the presence of members the female gender.

Rachna was surprised by the question that had come from nowhere. "There is one that starts outside the resort, but I haven't explored it myself," she told Rajat.

"I will go and check it out. Do you want to come?"

The introductions had continued as they slowly walked to the resort gates.

"Or maybe you want to do this tomorrow?" he had asked.

"No, thanks! I would rather sleep in. Besides, I don't have any experience with trekking."

"Sleep in? Don't you think this will be a good exercise? That's the problem with you doctors! You only enjoy dishing out advice, not following it yourself. You should try it."

The trek had been invigorating, and not as difficult as she had expected it to be.

She had been famished by the time they returned to the hotel, and had headed for breakfast.

It was at the breakfast buffet that her father and Rajat's father had recognised each other.

"Fancy meeting you here!"

"Yes, it has been so long!"

They had been course mates at the civil services training academy. Rajat's family had attended a wedding in Bombay, after which they had taken a detour to Matheran.

The next three days passed quickly, with both families spending most of the time together. Rachna and Rajat would keep chatting about their hostel experiences, while Mohit found quiet corners of the resort to write poetry. The adults would be busy exchanging notes on common friends and colleagues.

"I thought life in the hostel had prepared me for it but living alone in another country was quite a shock. Once I got used to it though, it was quite an experience," said Rajat, who was pursuing his Masters in engineering from Iowa. They enjoyed exchanging notes about their studies, student life in India and America, Rock bands, and Wimbledon.

"I am starting the final year of my course. Finding time to prepare for the exams will be a challenge," Rachna told him.

The classmates from the IAS Academy left Matheran with a revived friendship. Rajat returned to campus life in America. And Rachna found herself immersed in her studies and work again. Occasionally, they wrote to each other or tried to catch up over the phone.

Spending all her time at the hospital, she would tell him about her patients and the topics she needed to finish reading. "Rachna, at this rate, I will become a mix of a doctor and an engineer. You tell me so much about your studies!"

"That's because becoming a doctor needs more studying than becoming an engineer does! And these calls are so expensive, we can't afford to let them go waste while you struggle to put your thoughts together."

And they had laughed together.

Her chatty, voluble personality delighted him. A quiet person, he found this simple banter and ease of conversation comforting.

"The job offers are tempting, Rachna."

"Do you want to take them up?"

"No, I want to start my business in India. Mummy and Papa are building their house in Delhi. They will live there after Papa's retirement."

Like engineers, many doctors looked for opportunities abroad. But Rachna saw things differently. Her college life had given her a window not only into the world of medicine but also into the reality of the life of the underprivileged. She realised the many invisible advantages her privilege had given her and seen how deeply her life contrasted with that of the majority. In whatever modest way she could, she wanted to make a difference to the lives of the poorest.

Rajat's father had visited Bombay for work, and the friends had caught up again.

"So, how are the young men doing?" Rachna's father had asked Rajat's dad.

"Both are set to embark on their careers. Mohit has completed his accountancy degree and published his book of poetry. He will join the company Rajat is setting up in Delhi."

"Great! Nothing like having the family together."

"Yes, and Mohit has been Rajat's shadow, right from their school days."

"Rachna and Rajat seem to get along well. I was wondering if they are interested romantically in each other."

"I wouldn't mind at all if they are!"

"What do you think of a marriage proposal?"

"It's a good idea."

"Let's ask them."

His father had already discussed the idea with Rajat a few weeks ago. Rajat had been thrilled at the prospect.

The next time Rachna and he spoke, Rajat was silently brooding over some small thing, as usual. It was Rachna who brought up the crucial matter.

"Papa told me you are looking for a wife. You have lived alone in America for so long. I thought you would have found someone there."

"No, Rachna, I have been busy with my studies. Besides, I have always wanted to return to India, you know that."

"Yes, I know."

There was no reason not to proceed with the alliance. They enjoyed each other's company and understood each other. And the families knew each other well, too.

Both were busy with the culmination of their respective courses. The exams, coursework, and their busy routines kept them occupied. They were happy to leave the planning to the parents.

Mohit's wedding with Aditi had also been arranged; the two weddings were just a few weeks apart. The brothers would work together in Rajat's new company. New beginnings and happy tidings awaited the family.

Rachna had enjoyed the wedding rituals and ceremonies. Their extended families, colleagues, and all her friends had attended. Except for Venkat. Having finished his tenure in the hospital in Bombay, he had been preparing to leave for a training program in Australia.

She, on the other hand, had looked forward to exploring and settling down in Delhi.

"There is so much of Delhi that you haven't seen!" said Rajat.

She protested, "No, I have seen the Qutab Minar and the Red Fort. And India Gate, too."

He laughed. "You sound like a travel brochure! All that's the touristy part. We will explore the *real* Delhi together. I too have lost touch with those parts of Delhi that I used to frequent. The food in Delhi is awesome, and the shopping, too!"

"How come you know so much about shopping?"

"Oh! I used to wait for my girlfriends to finish their rounds in Janpath, Sarojini Nagar, and Karol Bagh," Rajat said.

"You are kidding! You proposed to me through your father! I can't imagine you with a *single* girlfriend, leave alone many!"

From Chandni Chowk to Khan Market, he had then detailed the gastronomic delights each place offered.

"You are such a foodie!" she cried in delight.

"Oh, I am! And you will understand why once you eat the nihari gosht for breakfast on Sunday."

Rajat had honed his cooking skills during his time in America. She, on the other hand, was more comfortable manoeuvring needles and probes into squirmy children than making an omelette. It would be fun learning to cook from Rajat.

The celebrations and revelry, along with the warmth that Rajat's family showered on the couples, outdid the cold of the foggy Delhi winter. The new year was all set to ring in a new life for them.

Rachna and Rajat escaped to the sunny beaches of Mauritius.

The trek to Treasure Island, the beach barbeques and the calm winds made it a place they would recommend to all other friends. They had already discovered common interests and hobbies. Now, they discovered each other. Rajat was caring and considerate. And shy. He would gently kiss her, beginning from the nape of her neck and moving lower down, reaching for her breasts and softly massaging them before taking them into his mouth. Slowly, tenderly, he kissed every part of her and then let her do the same to him. The gentle touch would continue, with his fingers running tiny circles on her body, and then he would enter her, waiting for her rhythm to match his. On more than one occasion, she had found him lost in thought afterward.

"What are you thinking about?"

"I hope you liked it."

The week sped by, and it was time to return. The warm sunshine of the coast would be replaced by the winter sun of Delhi. The leisurely walks by the beach with the waves frothing at their feet would give way to Rajat's long hours at the office, filled with audits and deadlines.

"Let's take off on a longer vacation, once things at work settle down," he said.

"Of course! In any case, I am planning to take a short break before looking for a job," she replied.

They had been packing the gifts they had bought for everyone. A T-shirt for Mohit, exactly like the one Rajat had bought for himself (a childhood tradition, Rajat had explained), scarves for his wife Aditi, and seashell souvenirs for their parents.

"I never realised you could be so shy! You brought this with us and didn't even tell me about it. This would have been interesting!"

The copy of *Kamasutra* had been hidden deep in his suitcase. He blushed.

"Never mind, we will have plenty of opportunities to try this out," she had reassured him with a teasing smile.

They returned to the traffic restrictions of the Republic Day parade in Delhi, and to a lot of paperwork awaiting Rajat in office. Rachna was looking forward to a life that was different from the routine of running to the hospital every day.

"Are you sure you won't get bored? I will be quite busy, and I don't think you have spent much of your life away from your patients," said Rajat the day after they arrived in Delhi.

"Yes, Rajat. I am looking forward to this. See, I have stocked up on cookbooks and movie DVDs. And, after a few weeks' break, I will begin applying for jobs."

That was how their new life unfolded. Until the family that had lovingly taken her in its fold was jolted by tragedy.

10

She had met Mohit only on a few occasions before her wedding. Two years younger than Rajat, he had studied business and accountancy. The brothers were close; they were often called the Ram-Lakhan of the family.

Both weddings, a new business, and Rajat's father's retirement made for a perfect family picture for everyone. Except that Mohit himself was missing. The suicide note, in which he had blamed only himself for his actions, did not help diminish the grief that descended on the family. Her in-laws had never imagined such a catastrophe and were shattered.

The family that had been blessed with happiness just a month ago was now stricken by sorrow. Rachna had seen tragedy and even death as part of her work, but this was a different kind of pain. The sadness was like an endless spiral, trapping the entire family in its vortex. Rajat's parents, of course, had been the hardest hit by the bereavement. Life had come to a standstill. It would be weeks before they would emerge from the numbness and gradually help each other cope. In those weeks, a strong bond of caring and concern developed between Rajat's parents and Rachna. She was grateful for the resilience and poise they showed. In turn, they drew strength from her caring company and affection. Together, they realised that they needed to make new decisions, big and small. Aditi, inconsolable in her grief, returned to Chandigarh with her parents—a decision everyone respected.

Rajat had been stunned into complete inaction. He hadn't resumed office and wasn't even taking calls. The factory needed him. *He* needed to get back to work, too.

"Returning to work will help you, Rajat," his father had advised him.

"Papa, the consultant position in Dubai is not a bad idea," Rachna had gently suggested. Maybe the change would help them deal with the unimaginable loss.

"Yes dear, that is what I am thinking, too," replied her father-in-law.

Rajat finally began to attend office, and she busied herself in helping her in-laws with their move to Dubai. From a family of six, abruptly, it was now just Rajat and her. But it actually felt like it was *only* her. It wasn't simply being alone in a large bungalow, or being away from her work and friends. There was something more. Rajat had changed. In a way that she couldn't quite put her finger on. It was as if she did not exist for him anymore. And, had never existed.

He was distant, reserved. Of course, he was grieving. But she couldn't understand the complete indifference he had begun showing her. Days would pass without his even acknowledging her presence.

Rajat found returning home from work painful. Memories of Mohit, and their time together, would surround him. He would shut himself away in his room, trying to escape them. In the process, he would shut out even Rachna. He had always had a short temper, but the rage he experienced now was unparalleled. It was directed at himself—and at everything around him.

He would fix his breakfast and leave for work. Returning late in the evening or even at night, carrying files and folders, he would head for the study. Throwing himself into work was his way of coping, she told herself. He would brusquely refuse her offers of tea. She would wait for him at dinnertime. But he wouldn't emerge from the study for hours. She would surf channels and drift off to sleep, not knowing when he would come upstairs. Each day was the same. Each week was the same. He was retreating deeper and deeper into himself. Her attempts to speak to him were met with indifference bordering on disdain. If she prodded him beyond a casual conversation, he would be enraged.

Deciding to resume work, she joined a small hospital. It did help her bring a routine to the day and pass a few hours in peace. But she remained hurt and confused about her relationship with Rajat.

"Rajat, the autos are on strike. Will you drop me at the hospital?"

As he was putting the car in gear, she had reached for his hand. The thinly veiled, disgust-like expression she saw on his face had stayed with her the entire day. It was similar to how he would recoil when she would sometimes reach out to him at night. That night, he came in a little earlier than usual, when she was taking in the 10 pm news. Picking up his pillow, his toothbrush and a few of his clothes, he had returned downstairs.

How could he explain the terrible sadness and guilt he was carrying inside him? How could he even dream of having a normal life after all that had happened? From the next day, he had not returned to their room, and she had seen even less of him.

She could find no reason for his indifference, rage or detachment from her. Something was very wrong, and there was no one she could share it with. Her pent-up feelings yearned for release, but there was no outlet to be found. Less than a year after marriage, having moved from one happy family to the other, one city to another, all she felt was despair that was beginning to consume her.

One monotonous evening, she came across the advertisement in a newsletter. The Global Children's Hospital had a vacant position for a Fellow in neonatology. Neonatology treated the tiniest of tiny babies, those that were not even a month old. Born premature, or with defects or some illness, they were fragile, and their survival, difficult. Attending to them needed the utmost sincerity, skill, and knowledge. But meeting the challenge and watching the babies thrive could be deeply satisfying, she thought.

The only problem was that the hospital was in Hyderabad. She had never anticipated moving away from Delhi, her new home—and from Rajat. But she had never anticipated a marriage with so much disconnect and distance, either.

That evening, she spoke to him about it.

"Rajat, there is an opening in a Neonatology fellowship." He had looked past her as he spoke a single word.

"And?"

"I was wondering if I should take it up. It is in Hyderabad. I want to know your thoughts about it."

"It's *your* fellowship. Why would *I* have any thoughts about it?"

And he had brushed past her into the study and slammed the door shut.

He was furious! How could she think of leaving him? Could she not understand what he was going through?

Upstairs, in the room into which he had welcomed her as a new bride, she burst into tears. Could he not understand how alienated and lonely she had been feeling all these months?

Sleep followed tears eventually, as it often does. She tried again the next day.

"Rajat, the fellowship is in Hyderabad. It is for over a year. We must discuss this before I decide about it."

"I don't see what I have to do with your work."

He had never felt so hurt. She had never felt so alone.

She sat there at the small table in the kitchen and reached for the application form.

It was more than six months since Mohit had committed suicide, and seven since their marriage.

It wouldn't be right to say that her in-laws had moved on. Recovering fully from the loss of their younger son was impossible. But they were trying to heal, to find purpose in other things.

Rajat too had found an outlet in his work. The company was doing well.

It was only she who seemed to have nothing to do; who was totally lost.

What had gone wrong in a marriage that was based on friendship that had transformed into love? What about the connection they had formed before their wedding and the intimacy they had shared in the first few weeks afterwards? Could Rajat be seeing someone else? Had he been having an affair since before they got married? If that was the case, why had he gone ahead with their wedding? Nothing made sense.

Joining the fellowship would help her get away from the suffocation she was feeling in this house and this marriage. The hard work would soothe her mind and blunt her pain.

For the second time in a year, she left for a new city.

11

The fellowship and the training associated with it were already underway when she joined. The duty roster, with everyone's initials, had already been posted. She would get to know her colleagues as she worked with them. She plunged into the familiar life of hospital studies, rounds and clinics once again. The duty hours were not as long as the ones during her previous training stint, but the work, especially in the neonatology Intensive Care Unit, was extremely demanding. This was a place where her tiny patients were obscured by the monitors, machines and tubes they were hooked up to. Where the doctors and nurses needed to be always alert and available.

It was on night duty one day in the ICU that a baby she had resuscitated was not stabilising. She paged the on-call doctor, who responded immediately.

With deft fingers and confident manoeuvring, he performed an emergency intubation and saved the little one. They sat watching the baby and the monitor. After a few moments, the bleeps of the machine became evenly spaced out, and the alarm stopped.

"Good you had kept everything arranged for the procedure," he told Rachna with a smile.

For a few moments, she didn't know how to respond.

Running into him here, after she had spent months in what seemed to be another universe, left her speechless. Her first reaction at seeing him enter the ICU was shock. But she could not utter a word or make out what he was thinking, because he got into a flurry of activity to save the child. *So the 'VR' on the duty schedule meant Venkat Ramakrishnan.*

The baby had drifted off to sleep, oblivious to how critically ill she had been, moments earlier. Venkat and Rachna signalled to the nurse and went to the tiny duty room at the end of the hallway.

He offered an explanation to her unasked question. "I joined as a faculty member a couple of months ago. The hospital has a strong community outreach program which appealed to me."

"I didn't know that. I joined just a week ago."

"How are you finding the training? I hope you have settled in?"

Someone from the canteen brought them tea. He poured it out in the stained cups that were always kept on the table in the duty room.

She sat on the bed and leaned her back against the wall.

"Yes, it's a great hospital."

Tea and the brief rest over, she returned to the ICU, and he, to his room. He had noticed the mangal sutra around her neck. But he was intrigued and disturbed by the fatigue in her eyes. It spoke of more than the tiredness of long working hours.

12

It was like old times again. The clinic overflowing with patients, spending hours reading medical journals, the hectic duty schedule and working with Venkat. The pattern of working hard together, helping each other out and lingering in the wards even after duty was over so they could discuss a case was also a familiar one. The only thing different was the sadness that obscured the shine in her eyes. Venkat noticed this. He refrained from asking her about the shadow that seemed to follow her all day. They continued with the routine they had fallen into.

About a week later, she was sitting in the cafeteria one morning, after a rough night's duty. She had waited in the queue outside the call booth and spoken to her parents. Listening to her mother update her about her friends, family and the city of Bombay seemed like mundane small talk. But it kept her anchored to life outside the hospital. Sometimes, after speaking to her parents, she would dial home. What else could she call it? The calls went unanswered most of the time. And even when Rajat would answer, the monosyllabic conversations lasted hardly a minute. They also left her feeling heavy-hearted.

She planned to use the day to finish doing up her room. It was almost a month since she had arrived, and she had not even set up her tiny hostel room. She needed to buy a bulb for the bedside lamp, wash and iron her kurtas, and arrange her books. Finishing the insipid mango shake, she was munching on her toast when he heard a voice.

"How have you been?" As always, Venkat's voice was soft and low.

The question caught her unawares. She had expected him to ask about one of the many babies they had been tending to in the ward.

Unwittingly, her eyes welled up. He changed the topic immediately. "Busy shift?"

"Yes."

He could see her eyes keep welling up.

"Come to my quarters for coffee," he suggested.

In all those years of working so closely with her, he had never imagined that he would invite her to his room. But, at that moment, he couldn't leave her alone. They had walked towards the faculty wing, which had larger rooms than the one she had been allotted. He opened the door to a large room that had a balcony. Thin curtains draped the windows. The three-drawer wooden desk had his papers neatly arranged. The lamp was like the one in her room, except that it worked. A bookshelf in a corner, a floor mattress with a printed bedsheet, and a study chair were the only other items in the room.

He guided her to the chair and fetched a glass of water from the kitchen. She could taste the earthen pitcher the water had been stored in. There was no place for him to sit, and she suddenly felt awkward.

"Some more, please."

They had known each other for years, but she realised that she knew nothing much about his personal life. She hadn't even thought about whether he lived alone. But it did seem like he did. This room led to a smaller room, where she could see a bed and a steel almirah. He returned with more water and found her sitting on the mattress he had laid out against the wall, lost in thought. He sat near her and handed her the water.

"You were applying to Australia for the position? I was sure you would get selected," she said.

"I did."

He had been heartbroken on hearing the news of her engagement to Rajat. Applying for the training program in Australia had been his way of distracting himself from his sorrow. He had attended the interview, but hadn't pursued the opportunity. Instead, he had moved to Hyderabad. Here.

He reached for the empty glass of water—but took her hand instead. She suddenly leaned into him and buried her face in his chest. He felt his shirt moisten just below the pocket. He continued holding her hand, and then pulled it gently and kissed it. Then he pulled her closer and found her cheeks and lips. Something stirred within her as she locked lips with him and pressed herself to him. He reached for her waist, locked his arms around it and continued to kiss her. She quivered and hesitated, just for a moment, before beginning to unbutton his shirt. He removed his hands and reached for her breasts, pushing her loose kurta up. For the briefest of moments, they paused, exactly at the same time. It was the moment when either of them could have chosen to pull away and not take things further. But the fleeting moment passed.

He felt the warmth and softness of her body as they explored each other on the thin mattress. She traced the outlines of his bones in the neck and felt him harden. The intensity of their kisses had been a prelude to their finding release in each other. Exhausted from work and feelings and life, she slept in his arms.

The single mattress, which was usually barely enough for Venkat's afternoon siesta, now had space for him to hold her in his arms. He slept, too. But it was a fitful sleep, one which he kept waking himself up from to check that this was not the dream he had dreamt ever so often.

When she woke up, she found that he was still holding her. He had draped a sheet over her and kept her clothes neatly folded at the foot-end of the mattress. She quietly got dressed.

"You can freshen up while I make you some coffee," he said softly, not giving her the opportunity to speak. She washed her face with cold water. She couldn't find the elastic band that held her shoulder length hair. She smoothened and combed her hair with her fingers.

He was waiting for her. He wanted her to hear what he had to say, before other thoughts and words began to occupy the space between them.

She averted his eyes, but allowed her to take her in his arms again.

"Rachna dear, I have loved you for so long. You found a place in my heart even when you were a hesitant medical student entering the children's ward for the first time. I would seek you out in a crowd of students or wait for you in the library. I would eagerly check the duty schedules, hoping we were posted together, and wished that our night duty together would never end. The fondness I had for you transformed into love somewhere on your journey from a tentative intern to a confident, mature paediatrician. But after Bombay, I never imagined I would see you again. Meeting you here made me realise that I have not forgotten my love for you. It is as strong as ever."

Leaving her with his words, he went into the kitchen.

Standing by the window, she took in the life outside. The lack of activity was not unusual for an afternoon on a hospital campus. Most people would be at work or in the library. Others would be getting some much needed rest after their long spells of duty. She heard him switch on the gas stove. The cylinders of the coffee filter clicked as they fitted into each other, and the aroma of coffee replaced the almost-burning smell of milk. Was the stillness of the sultry day making these sounds and smells seem exaggerated? Or was it because she felt surprisingly calm?

As if the noise of all that she was struggling with had finally died down.

When Venkat had confessed his feelings for her, she too had felt the gentle click of a missing piece of a puzzle falling into place. What he had said should have been a surprise. But it hadn't. She had always been aware of Venkat's silent presence in so many aspects of her life. In Bombay, they had spent so much time together—in the hospital, in the clinics, in the tiny canteen and in the library. She had felt closer to him than many usually do feel with their mentors. They had almost been kindred spirits in the hospital wards, working in silent synchrony, complementing each other. So how could she have not known he was falling in love with her?

She heard the *swish* of the freshly prepared beverage as he poured it into the tumblers. Her eyes followed him as he placed a tumbler of frothing coffee on the study table.

There was more he needed to say.

Gently touching her on her shoulder, he continued softly. "I know this is not something you imagined. And that you did not reciprocate my feelings."

He had fallen in love with her from the fringes of her life, but there could be no space for him in the centre. For her, he would be a friend, colleague, and a mentor. Nothing more. He had been sure of that.

They took their tumblers of coffee and returned to the thin mattress on the floor.

"All those years of being near you made me realise how far I truly was from you. And that that is the way it is meant to be. Having you as a part of my life, even in the smallest of ways, was all I could hope for, and it would have been enough for me. What happened between us today is something I never imagined or intended...."

He clasped her hands as she tried to find the words. If he didn't have the courage to finish what he had started, he would never forgive himself. "I will treasure every moment of this day forever, for there is nothing I have loved more than you."

Pulling him closer, she silenced him with a kiss.

When she had slept, he had been nervous about how she would react later. The ring on her finger reminded him of her wedding invitation from a year ago. She had been vulnerable today. Had he taken advantage of her vulnerability? Should he have stopped himself? Could *they* have stopped themselves? What next? He had forced himself to calm down. He needed to say all this to her. And she needed to hear it. How she would feel afterward was simply something he would have to accept.

They sipped their coffee, holding hands, sitting cross-legged.

The usually bubbly girl was quiet. But this was a different quiet. One that made her forget the disquiet of the previous year.

"You must be hungry. Like to go get some food? I've been rather busy since morning...didn't get a chance to cook."

"I would offer to cook, but I don't want to experiment on you! We can't have the best children's doctor falling sick!"

The spontaneity that had been missing since her first day at the hospital revealed itself and shone through. He smiled. And the smile grew broader.

They went out. It was her first trip into the city. But it felt like they had done this many times before. After a sumptuous biryani, they returned to the campus.

He stopped the bike opposite her hostel.

"You need to get some rest. Tomorrow, you are on duty again."

She returned to her small room, where she had laid out her things a few days ago. The room was like hundreds of others in hospital and medical college campuses everywhere.

It felt like the hostel rooms she had lived in before marriage. She felt like a college student or young trainee again—not held back by any weight or darkness as she attended to her work. The wedding, moving to a city far away, and life in the bungalow in Delhi—all seemed to have taken place a million years ago. Or had she just buried them deep within?

She spent the evening getting her notes organised for a presentation. She read the journals she had borrowed from the library. Then she reached for the latest edition of the textbook she had ordered and read it in the dim light before falling asleep, book by her side.

Two buildings away, Venkat cleared the steel tumblers and washed the coffee filter. On a usual day, Paati would come by in the evening. She would clean and attend to the laundry. Then she would make tea for him, flavoured with tulsi leaves from the plant that grew outside his window. But this was not a usual day. It felt magical, and he wanted the magic to last as long as was possible. He didn't want Paati or anyone else to be a part of his inner world right now. He decided to go out. Crossing the campus, he walked to the banks of the Hussain Sagar Lake. He walked around the lake, surrounded by couples, families, street children, beggars, bikes, and cars, oblivious to what he usually found chaotic.

When he returned to his room, he felt anything but alone. It was as if Rachna was still there, invisibly occupying the space around him. The research paper that needed to be reviewed and submitted sat on the desk. Ignoring it, he switched on the radio. Telugu songs he had heard in childhood filled the room. Humming along, he prepared to go to bed.

But he didn't go to the bedroom, where he slept every day. That night, he slept on the floor mattress; a deep, contented sleep.

13

The new routine was more fulfilling. He would finish his rounds and wait for her in the foyer or the canteen. She would complete her case records and bedside work. They would then go to his room, where she would sit at his desk, preparing for her submissions. He would wind up his chores and soak in her presence as he pored over the latest journals.

She noted the two bamboo chairs and small table that had appeared in a few days. She was impressed to see his dexterity in the kitchen, his thin, tapered fingers pouring the filter coffee from one steel glass to another, never spilling even a drop. It was the same mindfulness that he brought to his work. The same intense concentration that ensured that he picked up even the smallest of signs in the babies. She would leaf through his journals or read her textbooks. Sometimes, they would speak about the cases they had seen, or about the training schedule.

He spoke about how he was trying to establish a new community outreach program in the hospital. He didn't mention that he was also funding the program with more than half of his salary. She told him about her new home, and Delhi. She didn't speak about Rajat and the strange phase of turbulence that had pushed her away from life in that city. They discussed their patients, and how, even in a city that boasted of the best facilities, the health of the poor continued to suffer. Both believed that more needed to be done for the hundreds of thousands of poor children who didn't even get a chance at survival.

The discussions were always punctuated by filter coffee. And silence. The silence seemed to become him and his apartment. It had seamlessly expanded to include her. In the spartan room, with the comforting swishing sound of pouring coffee, she was beginning to find herself again. He understood, even before she did, that this silence would help her hear her own voice. That, whatever it was that was weighing her down, ran deep.

What they had come to share in this short time in Hyderabad was more than either of them had ever imagined possible. He would always be grateful for it. He had experienced enough in life to know that anything more would be a miracle. And it was stark realities and difficult decisions that made up his life, not miracles.

From time to time, the silence would be broken in a different way. Their tongues would find each other, and their lips would speak a different language. And, on the rare days that they were not on call, they would go out. Their favourite spot was by the lake. The buzz and activity there rejuvenated her. Seeing her enjoy street food and try to use the snatches of Telugu she had learned warmed his heart. Both of them would find their attention drawn by the street urchins playing with abandon or begging under coercion. They would wonder if these children even knew how poverty and lack of healthcare were affecting every aspect of their lives. Then they would talk about Venkat's dream to provide timely medical attention to such children. It was a topic that showed her a new side of Venkat. His eyes would light up, and excitement would make that quiet voice rise a few notches. She understood his feelings and admired his commitment to the cause.

14

The fellowship was coming to an end. Paperwork and submissions were added to their already-busy schedule. But, at the same time, it was time to celebrate and unwind. The department picnic was a tradition all the trainees looked forward to. After a lovely day of sightseeing, food and bonhomie, they returned, tired. She accompanied him to his room to pick up her books.

He pressed her close. "I will ask one of the trainees to mail you photos from today's picnic, along with the training certificate."

It was getting late. But she lingered. "Coffee?"

"Yes."

While he was making the brew, she used the few minutes to organise the thoughts that had been at the back of her mind for a few days. The familiar steel tumbler and brown liquid gave her the courage to not leave things unsaid.

"Venkat..."

"Rachna, you don't have to say anything if you don't want to."

"I know. But, I *do* want to!"

He sat, his back against the wall, sipped his coffee and waited.

"Venkat, I am going back day after tomorrow."

"I know."

"I did tell you about the events at home after my wedding..."

"Yes, what happened with Mohit was really unfortunate."

"Hmm. But, as you might have guessed, there was more. Things between Rajat and me were also not good."

He kept quiet.

"I am not sure how they will be now, once I return." He reached for her hand.

"Rachna, you haven't spoken much about all this for a year. What's on your mind now?"

"Venkat, whatever happened was overwhelming. For Rajat, for me, for everyone. There was so much pain, so much sorrow, that it touched everything. A lot of that heartache can never be fixed. I don't know if my marriage is one of the things those events damaged irreparably. Maybe it was collateral damage. But I need to find out. I need to give Rajat, and our relationship, one honest chance at revival. I don't know what the outcome of this will be, or even if *he* wants it, but it is something I must do.

"I understand."

"Venkat...please don't take this the wrong way. I care deeply for you. And your love for me is obvious even now, in those tears in your eyes."

"Rachna. I hear you. And, I *do* understand."

She realised then that he had known at the outset itself that things would be this way.

He continued talking. "You know I loved you in Bombay. And, I love you now—in Hyderabad. For you, the time we spent together in both the cities may have been different. But not for me. Both times, I loved you knowing that I could never have you. I never allowed myself even a sliver of hope. Go—to Delhi and your marriage. Do what you believe is right. Destiny will unfold its plans for you."

"And, for you."

"No, Rachna. Destiny usually leaves me out of its plans. It is something I should have got used to by now."

Back in her room, she ironed the saree she would wear for the graduation ceremony the next day. The day after that, she would be flying back to Delhi. If someone had asked her what she was feeling then, she wouldn't have been able to reply. She had come to Hyderabad feeling like a part of her had died. But now, she felt lighter; less burdened, though there was a lot that she still had to figure out.

She didn't know how things would unfold, but she felt more like herself now. Enough like the confident, young woman who took lifesaving decisions every day in the ward, who taught younger colleagues with aplomb, and who exuded confidence in her presentations.

Had she mistaken her feelings for Rajat? Did she even have a marriage to go back to? Was this how her life with Rajat would be forever? She would find the courage to look for, and face, the answers as they came.

After she left, Venkat was restless. He knew he would not see her again. Except at the graduation ceremony tomorrow, where they would be the teacher and the student again. This brief phase of togetherness was all he was destined for. He could feel it in his bones.

15

Delhi was cold, windy, and sunny at the same time. But it wasn't just the weather that made her shiver. When the chilly wind hit her on her face, it spelled out the question lingering in her mind. What about her marriage? And the life she had embarked upon with so much anticipation? Would it be like the Delhi she used to visit as a young girl—sunny, breezy, and colourful in the spring? Or, would it be the one in which she had arrived as a bride—chilly and frigid? Or, like the stifling humidity of the retreating monsoon when she had left for Hyderabad?

What was she returning to?

16

After she left for Hyderabad, Rajat had moved back into their room. In a strange way, he had felt relieved at being alone at home. But he began to feel his anger, guilt, and remorse all the more. He would wander to Mohit's room, sit there for hours and cry, sitting at his desk. Though his grief finally found some release, the other burdens would be his to carry for years.

When Rachna would call from Hyderabad, the conversation would be strained, almost formal. He understood her desire to pursue a career, but surely, she didn't have to abandon him at the most difficult of moments?

Gradually, he had come to terms with the reality that life, and he himself, had changed forever.

Going backwards in time was not possible, but he hoped that establishing the Mohit Foundation would help him come to terms with a future without the brother he had tried to shower unparalleled love on. The work of the organisation became his anchor, his way of keeping Mohit alive. Little parts of himself began to heal as the months had passed. The year of helplessness, hurting and healing had progressed. He began to understand that Rachna had been suffering her own pain, too. New to the family and the city, it could not have been an easy time for her.

As the months passed, he had realised that he had been consumed by his anger, which he had ended up directing at Rachna. She had tried to help him heal, but he had not been ready for it—or able to take her help. His suffering had its own journey and had affected everything, including their marriage. He wasn't sure where they stood as a couple now, but he knew it was a relationship worth trying to save.

Rachna had been surprised when Rajat had been home the last few times she had called. Even more so, when he had offered to come to Hyderabad to help her wind things up. "You must be busy with the factory. I too have a busy schedule here. I'll manage things," she had replied and given him the flight details.

He reached the airport in time for her flight. He zipped up his hoodie and waited for her. She stepped out, uncertainly scanning the crowd outside the terminal. He realised she was not sure if he would be there. He went to her and took her luggage.

"Papa and Ma are here for a few days. They were missing you, and decided to stay back until you returned," he said while loading her suitcase in the car. She had missed them, too. Also, she felt a twang of relief at not having to be alone with Rajat in the house, even if for just a while.

The warmth with which her in-laws welcomed her almost made her forget the chasm between Rajat and herself. The elders spoke of their experiences in Dubai and the places they had visited. She told them about the work in Hyderabad. Chatting late into the night, they played many rounds of rummy. It was a relief to see her mother-in-law looking healthier and her father-in-law involved with his work. In turn, they were happy to indulge her with warm ginger tea and gajar ka halwa.

A week later, they prepared to return to Dubai. But not before extracting a promise from her to visit them soon. She sighed as Rajat and she saw them off at the airport. As they returned home, she mentally prepared herself for the fact that Rajat would revert to his previous arrangement: moving back downstairs.

But he didn't.

17

A new routine developed, a testimony to how quickly we embrace change.

It was as if the fellowship in Hyderabad had been in another life; as if she had always been here, in this house—just Rajat and she. They began to share space—and life—with each other again. At first, they were guarded and tentative. Then, gradually, a little comfortable and trusting. It was the routine of a couple. A newly formed couple in some ways, but a couple, nevertheless. The excitement of the wedding and the darkness of the marriage were things of the past. There was a stillness now. Not an uncomfortable one, but not a deeply satisfying one, either. If the hostility and detachment that had stung her earlier were absent, so were the exuberance and light-heartedness with which Rajat had courted her.

He was more serious now; would brood more often. Yet, he was also attentive to her; warm and considerate in an almost—but not quite—formal way. She attributed it to the loss the family had suffered and held space for him. Rajat seemed most comfortable at work or when talking about it. She joined a new corporate hospital near their home. The Mohit Foundation that Rajat had set up as the Corporate Social Responsibility arm of his company was the only mention he ever made of Mohit, the tragedy, or their relationship from those days. The wheels of her household, and her life, resumed rolling slowly. And, she hoped, smoothly. As she and Rajat began once more to share space and the routine acts that make up a marriage, it was the external that began to recover first. Their emotional intimacy would take longer to be restored.

It had been a busy day at the hospital.

"The rattling sound in your car had to be fixed. So I have left it at the service station. I will pick you up."

On the way home, he gently suggested, "Why don't you think about starting your own clinic? I think you always wanted to do that, right?"

She was surprised that he remembered.

"Also, I was wondering if we could set up a children's hospital as part of the Mohit Foundation. We could set it up near the factory. It would help the workers and their families. Can you take charge of this project for me?"

The 'for me' that he had added so hesitantly—almost inaudibly—touched her. She almost reached out for his hand.

"That's a great idea. Of course!"

They chatted about the idea all the way home, and as she reheated the food from the refrigerator. Rajat would usually lay the table. And they would speak about their day as they ate. Then his fax messages would begin to come in, and she would clear up the kitchen. Back upstairs, she would drift off to sleep watching a soap opera. Meanwhile, he would catch up on reading in the armchair.

That day, however, he was already in bed.

"Tired today?"

"Hmm, no."

He was as shy and tentative as on their honeymoon.

Initially caught unawares when he turned towards her, she slowly responded to his touch. As he gently traced his hand along her thigh, she caressed his chest and found his lips. Slow, gentle and unhurried, it was like their honeymoon all over again. They found release in each other, together. Later, they fell asleep. They held each other through the night, as if each feared losing the other again.

18

Maybe each one of us must go through some turbulent phases, she thought. This was probably inevitable in the ebb and flow of life. She just hoped that *this* particular phase was behind them for good.

Rajat planned her hospital with the same dedication he showed to his work. Her clinic in Delhi and the hospital on the outskirts of Bahadurgarh gave her a lot of satisfaction. The years passed quickly. Like the firm and the hospital, the family grew. They devoted themselves to creating the life they wanted and enjoying the life they created. How or why the darkness had descended upon them was not important. What *was* a fact was that, when it had finally lifted, it had not left its shadow behind.

Occasionally, she did think about Venkat, especially when she visited Paalna. She was sure he would have shared her enthusiasm for the project. He kept sending her a signed copy of each of his books. His photo would be printed on the back cover of each book. The information that accompanied the picture was precise and clinical, and pertained only to his career. It didn't capture his dedication towards setting up health centres in villages or his passion for community service. As the years passed, the memories of the time they spent together morphed into respect for the wonderful, gentle person who had stepped into her life when she had needed him the most.

In their months together in Hyderabad, he had never pressured her to speak about her relationship with Rajat. Intuitively, he had known that she was struggling with so much. She knew he loved her tremendously. A future with her would have meant the world to him. Yet, he never even spoke about it. After confessing his love for her, he had never again mentioned the matter. He had known, as had she, that she would return to Delhi—and Rajat. Not expressing his love time and again had itself been his way of showing love. And, in recent times, he had followed her career and kept in touch with her—but very professionally, never intruding in her life or space. She wondered if he had married. She could only imagine the tenderness and affection with which he would raise his family. She hoped that, like her, he too had built his little nest to cherish; that he had found someone to care for and to be cared by.

Other than his books, this letter was the first time Venkat had contacted her after she left Hyderabad. He had written to her about the dream he had shared with her all those years ago; a dream she too had believed in. Reading the letter, she had immediately shared his happiness and pride. Of course, it would be a great opportunity to attend the inauguration. Paalna too would benefit from the initiative. She had decided to attend the ceremony. She had begun to fill up the form, but had been called for an emergency in the clinic just then.

However, before she could return to the form the next day, Rajat's strange behaviour had begun. At first, he seemed distracted and nervous. She had felt that he was ill at ease, especially around her. And then, he had begun those oblique references to Venkat, Paalna, and telemedicine. It was strange, and had made her uncomfortable. Did he know about her brief liaison? Had the past come back to bite her now? Each time Rajat would bring up the topic of the new hospital, she feared it would cloud her future. *Their* future. And she did not mention Venkat's letter to Rajat.

19

Present Day

Rachna was surprised to hear the doorbell. She was even more surprised to see Rajat there. She stepped aside to let him enter. His jaw was taut, and face muscles tense. The strange way in which he was looking at her unnerved her. She composed herself. She was sure that he suspected her affair with Venkat. She was no closer to figuring out how. She reminded herself that the consequences of his discovery were more important than how he had found it out.

She waited for him to speak. She would let him talk, ask, vent. Whatever happened after that, they would cross it when it happened. The fire inside him seemed to be scorching him. He would continue to fan it, even at the cost of burning himself and those around him. This was Rajat at his most intense and mercurial.

"We must link our hospital to this network. You should go for the inauguration today, so we know more about the whole thing." He picked up the newspaper and stared at the ad.

Her heart skipped a beat. She waited for her quickened pulse to settle down.

"Sure, we can explore it."

I have a meeting near the venue. I could drop you there and pick you up an hour later."

"Hmm."

There was no point in arguing. She went upstairs to get ready.

She didn't feel the softness of her silk saree against her fingers as she pleated it and pinned it in place. Instead, she felt as if Rajat's eyes were boring into her, though he was not in the room. She looked into the mirror to tie her hair into a topknot. The plum-coloured lipstick complemented the string of rubies Rajat had gifted her on her birthday.

To be able to have the conversation Rajat was leading her towards, she needed to straighten out her tangled emotions. She needed to silence that nagging, recurrent thought: *What if he knew about Hyderabad and her affair? What would he do if he found out her lie?*

She sternly replied to the nagging thought: *There is no lie. Our marriage is the only truth. Nothing else matters. At least, I hope that's how Rajat would see it.*

He couldn't take his gaze off her when she came down the stairs, the saree from Sanvi's mundan ceremony still as good as new. She looked radiant in that deep shade of pink. The hint of kajal, the round bindi, and the rose-gold watch with its large dial completed her formal look. He froze. Despite himself and all that had transpired in the last few days, he was spellbound. She looked elegant and beautiful, as she often did. But it was more than that. She looked *vulnerable*. Like she had looked in her ribbed sweater and jeans at the airport when she had returned from Hyderabad. She also looked buoyant and carefree, as in the hotel lobby in Matheran, all those years ago. She looked confident, like she had when they had rushed Pranav to the hospital to treat his fractured arm. It seemed as if all the roles she had played in his life—friend, lover, confidante, wife—had come together in the simple act of her walking down the stairs.

She looked into his eyes. "I am ready."

He needed to silence the hammering in his head.

∞

He started the car, and she reached for his sunglasses. Wiping them before passing them to him was one of the many ordinary, everyday things they did for each other. He paused for a second, then took them from her and reversed the car.

As they drove, he asked her, "Venkat was your teacher, right?"

"Yes. And mentor too, during my MD," she said, nodding.

"Quite a number of books he has written."

"Yes, they are the best textbooks for students and practitioners. And, he was a faculty member when I did the fellowship in Hyderabad."

There! She had let it drop. "Ohh…"

"Rajat, is everything ok? You have been very stressed out, lately."

"Yes, Rachna, you are right. I have had a lot on my mind, but it is beginning to get sorted, finally."

Their favourite melody *'Tumko dekha toh yeh khayal aaya, zindagi dhoop tum ghana saaya'* played on the radio, but neither of them hummed along.

Rajat stopped the car outside the gates of the auditorium. "Will pick you up in an hour."

He drove towards the highway and parked off the road. He had been right about everything. He was sure of it now. How could their entire life be based on a lie? Rachna's secrets could destroy their marriage. This wasn't fair. Why had she done this to them?

But, through the insistent hammering in his head, he could feel a feeble voice making itself heard. It grew stronger by the moment. Had he always been fair to her? Even if she had had an affair with Venkat, could he really blame her for it? Hadn't he been the one who had distanced himself from her first, that too, for no fault of hers? Hadn't he kept secrets from her? What about those days when *that* tragedy had shaken all of them?

He had been as excited about their wedding as about his new company. Entrepreneurship came naturally to him, and he had been committed to starting operations as early as possible. There had been a few glitches in the early days, which could have been avoided. But they had been busy with the wedding ceremonies, he had reasoned to himself. He had planned to focus on the audit reports once they returned from the honeymoon. Mohit's training in accounts, and his work experience, would help in this. It would be a good idea for the brothers to work together.

The first time he had questioned the wisdom of that move was when an important contract Mohit had been handling suddenly fell through. Then, the mismatched entries had come to his notice. They would need to devise a process for the accounts and course-correct, he had thought.

Rajat and Mohit had clashed on other occasions, too. He had observed a pattern of irregularities in the annual accounts statement. All the transactions that didn't add up were Mohit's. The discrepancies were minor, but they were a breach of trust. He was furious. Mohit had asked him for advances, and he had approved a few. If Mohit had needed more money, he should have been upfront about it, instead of stealing from the company!

It was typical of Mohit not to be grateful for Rajat's offer that he join the company. In fact, he had been quite disinterested in learning the ropes. He had not shown much enthusiasm for his own marriage, either. He had always been unsure about his decisions and inconsistent with his plans. Rajat could never understand why Mohit couldn't be more like him. He, a go-getter, had been irritated by his brother's ambivalence. Was Mohit's jealousy rearing its ugly head, leading him to sabotage his brother's fledgling firm?

A confrontation was inevitable.

That evening, after everyone else had left office, he had called Mohit to the conference room. "What is the meaning of this? You have been stealing from my firm! I should have known better than to allow someone like you to be a part of it."

"*Your* firm, Bhaiya? You always said it is *our* firm! Shows how you really feel about it. Typical of you; entitled as always! You have always got whatever you wanted. I am tired of living life in your shadow. Sick of living up to *your* imaginary benchmarks based on *your* achievements."

"We will talk about whose firm it is, later on. You are jealous of me. You've had trouble holding on to whatever jobs you found."

"Bhaiya! Don't poke your nose in my affairs. I have done nothing wrong. Surely, I too have the right to live life the way I want? To do the work that gives me satisfaction? I have no interest in manufacturing pumps and pipes, unlike you."

"That's fine. It's not a matter of what interests you and what doesn't! These papers are proof that you have been embezzling money since you joined the firm."

"Yes Bhaiya, I have. I had no choice. You rejected my requests for money. Then you convinced Papa that I was up to no good. It wasn't fair to me that Papa supported *your* dreams but not mine. You were not even willing to be my guarantor for a loan. I wanted to start my own ecommerce platform, but you had already decided that it would be a failure. I was sure my company would do well and that I would have returned your money."

Shocked and seething at Mohit's defiance, Rajat had struck him on the face.

It was true that his brother had seemed motivated by his ecommerce idea. But, like always, he had chosen such a vague business idea. Rajat had not been convinced. His words to their father rang loud in his mind. "Papa, it is a very new field. And the idea seems shaky. We don't know if it will work or not. It's another example of Mohit's flight of ideas."

Mohit needed to become more responsible. He was always dreaming about things. All his interests, like his poetry, were so abstract and flaky! How could he think of launching his own company?

"At least, you could have given me an opportunity to prove myself," hissed Mohit.

"Mohit, you have always been a loser. You would have lost the money—and your reputation. Stop giving excuses for stealing my money. You are not just a loser; you are a thief, too," Rajat spat out before screaming and leaving the conference room.

It had taken him some time to get a grip on his temper. After all these years, Mohit had finally shown some initiative. Perhaps he *did* deserve another chance. He could start his venture on a small scale while continuing to work at their firm. If the ecommerce venture didn't work out, he would have this company and job to fall back on.

The light in Mohit's chamber at the other end of the corridor had been on when Rajat left the office. Ordinarily, he would have stopped there before leaving. But, not risking his temper again, he had decided to speak to his brother in the morning.

He was still groggy when Rachna shook him awake.

The police were all over the apartment; they had cordoned off Mohit's room. People around him were rushing, shouting, talking. But for him, it was like a movie on fast-forward without an audio track. Someone with gloved hands showed him a suicide note. The words *thief*, *ecommerce* and *loser* sprang up at him. It seemed as if they were screaming *killer*. Neighbours and relatives had begun to arrive. Everyone kept murmuring the words *suicide*, *tragedy*, *depression*. To Rajat, all those sounded like *killer*, too. He wished the police would handcuff him and lead him away. He had killed his brother.

No one knew what exactly had happened. Mohit had written about his shattered dream of running an ecommerce company and his love for his family. But he had not written anything about what had happened that evening between the two brothers.

Rajat had been numb with grief. And, guilt. He had retreated deep within himself. His rage and frustration had been directed at everyone around him, especially Rachna. Suffering in his own hell, he had become cold and indifferent to her. After pushing his brother to take that extreme step, what right did he even have to be alive, leave alone, lead a happy life?

His parents had coped by leaving for Dubai. And he? Alternating between ignoring his wife and raging at her had become his way of coping. Rachna had been caught in the cauldron of his thoughts. He was ashamed of his behaviour, but was not able to stop himself from alienating Rachna. For no fault of hers, he had pushed her away. But he wouldn't have blamed her so much if she had decided not to go to Hyderabad at just that time.

In the years that had followed, little by little, he had allowed himself to feel his pain and mourn all that he had lost. Time, and his family's love, had mended him enough to face life again. The nightmares had decreased over the years; the flashbacks seldom troubled him now. But he knew that there were parts of him that had been broken and would never heal. While he had managed to lay some of his demons to rest, some others would always be a part of him. The consequences of his anger and impulsive behaviour would plague his family forever.

His mind fast-forwarded to that day at the airport, when Rachna had returned from Hyderabad. Dressed in jeans, pullover and sneakers, she had looked like the girl he had first met in Matheran. An aloof, distant stranger. But a *vulnerable stranger whose eyes still held hope.* A stranger he wanted to have in his life.

He had known then that he had to try and mend their relationship. He only hoped she would let him try.

In the time since she had returned from Hyderabad, trying to rise beyond his guilt and shame, he had inched forward. To life with Rachna. And he had been able to do what he had never imagined: rebuild his life, nurture his family again and devote himself to home and work, even if tentatively, and only to some degree. The sunshine of their love had given them strength to weather the storms and endure the droughts that are part of every couple's journey. But all this wouldn't have been possible without Rachna's compassion for him. Without judging him, she had allowed him to grieve and try to heal. And even when he kept shunning her, she had been there for him. As if waiting for him to return to himself—and her.

Rajat sat in his car, lost in thought. Even today, he held the secret of Mohit's death close to his heart. Yes, it was far back in the past, but it couldn't be denied that he had never shared those events with anyone—not even with *her*. And after that, in spite of her repeated attempts to help him and find out the cause of his sorrow and anger, he had kept pushing her away. Had he been fair to her?

Even after Rachna had returned from Hyderabad, it was she who had given him the space and time to rebuild their relationship. Her patience, composure and understanding were the basis of their love and marriage. Whenever self-doubt would question him, he would look to her for the answers. And find them. He valued her more than anything else in the world. After those difficult first few years, they had worked hard to build and nurture their relationship. That was how their love had grown: in the spaces of routine life; in the usual acts of companionship, finding meaning in the mundane.

The lives they lived today were a result of all those efforts. In a life that could had peppered with uncertainties, she had always been his absolute.

20

The hammering in his head finally stopped. He lifted his head from the steering wheel and looked around after what seemed like ages. The world outside the car looked cheerful once again; the fog seemed to have lifted. With Mohit, he had let his anger and ego get the better of him, destroying many lives in the process. He couldn't do it again. Not with Rachna.

Rachna, today, and their life together. These were the only truths.

There was nothing he wanted to know about her yesterday; not if it could threaten their today or tomorrow.

It was time to pick her up. He reversed the car.

She opened the door and smoothened her saree as she sat in the car. Rajat looked tired. *He must check his blood pressure,* she thought.

"Do you have any appointments now?"

She was surprised. More questions. She replied guardedly, "No."

"We could go out for ice cream, if you are not in a hurry. It has been so long." And he smiled. A genuine, heartfelt smile after ages.

Relief and happiness bubbled up from within her and mingled in her laughter.

"Of course!"

"But today, both portions will be of your choice," he said.

She turned up the volume on the radio and sat back as the liquid notes of '*Hothon se choo lo tum, mera geet amar kar do*' filled the car—and their hearts.

∞

Humraaz

Humraaz – Confidante

Wherever you are, and whatever you do, be in love.
—Rumi

1

Present Day

The sedan slowed as it weaved through the stream of traffic. After a busy week, Mahima was looking forward to a relaxed day. The merger deal with the Australian delegation had finally come through yesterday. The achievement made the Family Day celebrations scheduled for this evening extra-special. Mahima smiled as she reached for the newspaper Reshma had packed in her jute bag.

Reading the newspaper on the way to work was an old habit. There was a time when each section of the newspaper had had its own relevance. After taking in the news, she would linger on the smattering of advertisements. She would use her red sketch pen to circle the relevant classifieds. The assurance of health, wealth or fortune that the weekly horoscope contained seemed to be meant especially for her. But these days, the headlines had already been 'broken' by many competing news channels. Live weather updates were available on everyone's phone. And Zodiac sign-based predictions had been usurped by new entrants to the world of prophecy, like tarot and numerology. Even the editorials were watered-down versions of the incisive commentaries of the olden days that would be intensely discussed in coffee houses amidst acrid fumes of cigarette smoke. The comic strips were the only part of the newspaper that offered any novelty now.

But, bound by habit, she continued her ritual every morning on the way to work. Wasn't that typical of all our habits? Vestiges of our past, which we are too lazy or too sentimental to change; we kept repeating them until they became a part of us—our routine—and our subconscious, without our knowing why.

She took her eyes off the newspaper and looked out the window. People were rushing about with a sense of purpose. Most of them would be headed to their workplaces. She often wondered how the city kept expanding to make space for the thousands who came here by choice or compulsion, in hope or in desperation. But it did. Just as it had for her when she had arrived here as a shy bride, 25 years ago. From rushing to catch a rickety DTC bus then to being driven in a shiny Mercedes now, so much in her life—and the city of Delhi—had changed.

She remembered how the ambling traffic used to be dwarfed by the double-decker buses, instead of by the metro that now whizzed above the chaos of perpetually honking vehicles. There were swank malls everywhere, and so many shiny glass towers. New slip roads and flyovers had been constructed, their beautiful landscape coexisting with the clusters of shanties that inevitably cropped up below them. Yet, the greenery of the city remained, as did its quintessential blend of history and modernity that made Delhi, *Delhi*.

Like the newspaper, her destination—the corporate office of Roxanne Industries—had remained constant over the years.

She quickly skimmed over the headlines. Until a photo inside caught her eye.

Sanjay.

2

It was a recent picture from a corporate event. The report was headlined:

Sanjeevani Pharma Research Institute announces breakthrough cancer treatment drug

She smiled. The dreams Sanjay had tried so hard to bury had flowered, just as she had known they would. Their roots had run deep, after all.

The car drew up at the foyer of one of the most famous buildings on Kasturba Gandhi Marg, the top of which housed a revolving restaurant with panoramic views. The offices of Roxanne Pharmaceuticals occupied the entire fourth floor of the building.

The valet opened the door for her, and she smoothened the creases of her crisp cotton saree. Slipping the newspaper into her jute bag, she entered the elevator.

The mood in the office was festive, with everyone greeting and congratulating her.

"Ma'am, the merger is such a great achievement!"

"Did you see the coverage on TV yesterday?"

"Ma'am, you single-handedly lifted the share market yesterday. What a rally!"

She smiled. "Thank you. But it is the efforts of all of you that make the company what it is. We will all celebrate together in the evening."

The deal with the Australian delegation was another feather in the company's cap. Roxanne Pharmaceuticals had become the first Indian pharma company to acquire an international chain of companies. She entered her chamber and called for the draft of the press release.

Having made the necessary corrections and authorised the release, she sank into the couch upholstered with blue fabric. The large bay window seat overlooking the bustling road was her favourite spot for both, brainstorming and quiet reflection. This entire room was close to her heart. She had designed it, along with the logo of the firm and the rest of the office space. She had spent hours poring over the architect's plans and ideating with the interior designers when the office was being built. The colours of the brand were reflected in the pristine white desk and chair, and the blue wallpaper.

She unfolded the newspaper at the page with the grainy photograph. She didn't need to wear the reading glasses that hung on her neck on a silver chain to sharpen the details that the low printing quality had made fuzzy. The mole near his upper lip, the furrows on his forehead and the prominent Adam's apple stood out, as always. So did the scar running along his left jawline. Once her mind had taken in all this, she peered at the caption below the picture.

The announcement was made at the annual convention of the Federation for Drug Research and Discovery.

Sanjay was flanked by the Chairperson of the Chambers of Indian Pharmaceuticals and the Vice-Chancellor of a new university.

Memories of the days when Roxanne was a single-room office in a corner of this building came alive. What had started as a small manufacturing plant on the outskirts of Delhi was now a township with a large on-site community of workers and their families. Sanjay was a luminary in drug research and she, the CEO of Roxanne Pharmaceuticals. Neither of them had ever imagined the lives they were living today.

Just as she began to read the news report, there was a knock on the door.

"Ma'am, these documents came in just now." Her reverie would have to wait.

The urgent documents had sections marked for her comments. She reached for the phone to issue a few instructions.

Arjun, one of their longest-serving employees, waited to take the papers back from her.

"Arjun bhaiya, all set for the evening? You must bring your grandson along."

"Ji, ma'am. Already bought new clothes for him. This is his first outing," the elderly man said with a broad smile.

He shut the door softly behind him, leaving her with Sanjay's picture again. And the memories.

3

1993

The interview was scheduled for 10:30 am, and Mahima was worried that she was late. The rickety DTC bus had dropped her off at the other end of the road and she rushed across Agrasen Ki Baoli to RK Towers, one of the few high-rise buildings around Connaught Place.

She needn't have worried about being late. The waiting room was packed with candidates, and only those with experience were being shortlisted for the interview. Once more, she would have to return home and be the target of Pawan's caustic remarks.

Big cities work differently. Inexperienced people like you don't stand a chance here. Pawan's words rang in her ears as she entered the elevator.

In the dim fluorescent light, the handwritten piece of paper stuck on a side panel of the elevator caught her eyes. "Wanted, Accountant. Freshers can apply. Roxanne Industries. 4th Floor."

She quickly pressed 4 instead of G. *May even be an old advertisement,* she thought. Exiting the elevator on the fourth floor, she saw a small sign outside one of the rooms: Roxanne Industries.

She knocked on the door that stood ajar. A male voice answered, "Come in!"

She walked in to find a cluttered office that contrasted with the plush air-conditioned office she had left behind moments ago. There were four tables and two chairs, a filing cabinet and a pedestal fan that seemed more useful than the slow, decrepit one on the ceiling.

At the biggest of these tables, seated behind a stack of papers, and with calculators and a typewriter laid out before him, a stocky gentleman, probably in his early thirties, was scribbling furiously. Shirt sleeves rolled up to his elbows and his forehead furrowed, he didn't look up from the sheet on which he was writing and crossing out something.

"Excuse me?"

"Yes?"

"You need an accountant?"

"Hmm, yes."

"I have completed my Intermediate CA. I have not worked anywhere, but..."

She held out a Xerox copy of her one-page CV and waited to see his response.

"Can you start tomorrow?"

She was taken aback. *That's it?* she wondered incredulously. But she was relieved, too.

She had wondered if he would object because she had completed only the Intermediate level of CA.

"Would you like to see my certificates?"

She held out her folder, but he had gone back to his registers.

"Will you be able to maintain ledgers? And organise previous bills? There is a lot of pending work here."

She recalled the many evenings sitting on the white *gadda* (floor mattress) with her father in his saree shop and closing the accounts for the day.

"Yes, I can."

"Tomorrow. Or the day after? Not beyond that."

Back home, she wondered if he had been serious. He had certainly seemed to be.

As she rolled the dough for dinner, Pawan remarked, "So, another failed interview today?"

"Actually, I got a job."

She described the events of the morning.

"He didn't give you an appointment letter? You are so naïve. You don't even know if it is really a proper company."

Pawan had strengthened her doubts, and she didn't go back to Roxanne the next day.

The day after, however, she somehow convinced herself to go. She told herself it might be her only chance at getting a job despite her lack of experience. If things didn't work out, she could always come back home.

She finished the poha she had made for breakfast and rushed to the bus stop. She didn't want to be late for work. When she reached the office, the gentleman was at the desk, and the fan was whirring away. It was only 9:30 am. The black pen, the sheet with his annotations and the furrow on his forehead were exactly as they had been two days ago.

This time though, he gave her more than a cursory look. "You can take that table."

He pointed to the one farthest from his and returned to making notes.

She hung her handbag on the back of a chair and moved the files aside.

He walked over and handed her a file marked 'Bank' and two envelopes labelled 'Bills'. He then handed her a large plain envelope, which she assumed contained her appointment letter. It didn't. It was a copy of the bank hypothecation papers.

Maybe this was a mistake, after all? she wondered.

There was nobody else in the office except for the two of them. She didn't know what was expected of her—the hours she was to put in, or even how much she would be paid. *What kind of a firm was this?*

She began to make notes from the file and realised that the accounts were as much of a mess as the office space was.

The sound of an electronic typewriter filled the room.

She began arranging the bills chronologically. After some time, he walked up to her with a typewritten letter on the company's letterhead. She glanced through it.

Sanjay Shukla, Director of Roxanne Industries, had appointed her, Mahima Mathur, as Junior Accountant, at a salary of Rs. 950/- per month.

"Most offices around here work from 10 to 5. You can do that, too. The other staff is usually busy onsite, at the factory."

After a brief pause, he softly added, "Salary might be delayed."

He moved the pedestal fan from his corner of the room to somewhere in the middle and plugged it in. It whirred to life and provided them whiffs of air by turns. She quickly adjusted the paperweights on her table and returned to work.

4

The office didn't seem to have any working hours. Sanjay would be there before she arrived. The 'others' he had mentioned on his first day were Kailash, who was often travelling to client meetings, and Som, who spent most of his time at the factory, riding from one crisis to the other. Kailash's train tickets, which he submitted for reimbursement (but without his food bills), were a reminder of the shoestring budget the firm was operating on.

Roxanne was a firm in trouble.

She started each day by poring over the bills and other papers. She made lists of all the vendors and verified each entry before authorising payment vouchers. Like clockwork, the boy from the tea shop would silently leave cups of tea at her desk at 11 am and 3 pm. For lunch, she would slip off to the common canteen on the ground floor to have the chapatis and subzi she had packed for herself in the morning, accompanied with a chilled Maaza. The afternoons would melt into evenings.

At 5 pm, she would pick up her handbag, hung on the back of her chair. She would remove her dupatta from the nail on the wall where she hung it in the morning and switch off the oscillator of the pedestal fan before leaving. Sanjay would look up from his desk, acknowledge her departure with an imperceptible nod and return to his work. She would take the bus back to her two-room home often carrying a bundle of files with her to study on the way. She would reach home just a few minutes before Pawan. A few precious minutes in which she stopped at the first-floor house of Gayatri aunty to pick up Piyu and drain the cardamom tea aunty kept ready for her.

Sanjay and Mahima's routine of working in silence changed somewhat whenever Kailash was in office. Kailash, who enjoyed his role of the affectionate elder, filled her in with details about the company. Kamal Pandit, whose photograph hung on the wall behind Sanjay's desk, had been Kailash's elder brother. He had set up the company after he was forced to leave Kashmir in the face of escalating violence in 1990. Those days, the firm had manufactured active pharmaceutical ingredients to supply to drug companies for use in their medicines. Kamal had named the firm after the Anglo-Indian woman whose beauty had mesmerised him enough to renounce his orthodox Brahmin family. Roxanne had been his lover, muse, and wife. The gentleness of their romance, and their brief life together, had been interrupted by her schizophrenia. The firm was his tribute to her after she died from an overdose of her medication. It was to also be *her* legacy to their young daughter Neena.

Beautiful and reticent, Neena was coveted by many men in college. But she had eyes only for her senior, Sanjay, who was pursuing a PhD. He was an excellent student, a committed researcher, and a dreamer. Sanjay dreamt of discovering new drugs and making better medicines. Their budding romance, the busy schedules at college and their dreams of the future had kept the young couple occupied and happy, without much to worry about. That is, until tragedy struck.

The plane in which Kamal Pandit had been travelling had crashed. There had been no survivors. It was an unexpected end to Sanjay and Neena's uncomplicated, happy college life. Neena was devastated. Shock made her withdraw into a cocoon of denial. Sanjay had tried hard to share her sorrow, but her sadness had continued to debilitate her. "Neena, returning to college and finishing your degree will help you. That's what your father would have wanted."

With great difficulty, he had managed to get her to resume college. He was occupied with completing his own degree and helping Neena prepare for her exams. Kailash had taken care of the rudderless firm into which Kamal had poured all his dreams, energy, and money.

Almost a year later, Neena passed her final year exams and Sanjay completed his PhD. Attending his convocation had been a matter of pride for his parents.

"We would have liked to meet Neena, too," his mother had remarked.

"Yes, mother, but she isn't keeping too well. It has been a difficult year for her."

"I can understand. Give her our love."

Giving him and his plans their blessings, they had returned to Banaras, where his father was a professor at Banaras Hindu University.

Immediately after seeing them off at the railway station, Sanjay had rushed to Neena's house with the rolled-up degree certificate. He had been waiting for this moment since he had received the letter of acceptance from the university in Germany. The post-doctoral position in a top-ranking university would take him one step closer to his career in drug research, an ambition he had shared passionately with Neena in the three years they had been together.

He planned to join the position and return to India for their wedding a few months later. Meanwhile, Neena could work with Kailash to complete the pending orders and paperwork for the inevitable dissolution of Roxanne.

He found Neena in her father's study, looking over the incorporation documents of Roxanne. It was a relief to see that she wasn't her usual doleful self. Usually, he would find her somewhere in the veranda, lost in her thoughts, her painting canvas untouched and the tubes of paint unopened. But today, seeing her petite self in her father's large chair, taking notes on the Roxanne letterhead, he felt a glimmer of hope. *Perhaps this was a sign, and a new beginning was on the anvil?*

It was, though in a way he had not expected. He took the chair opposite hers.

"It is good to see you at your father's desk," he said with a smile.

"Yes, I have been thinking about the company."

She poured him some kehwa from the flask on her desk.

"How was the convocation?"

"Lovely. I missed you there. Hope you are feeling better now."

"Sanjay, let's get married. Immediately. We can start a new life, filled with hope and happiness."

Bewildered, he struggled for words. Her enthusiasm should have made him happy, but there was something ominous about this.

"You, me, and Roxanne. Our new life."

This was a surprise to him. Whenever the topic had come up, Neena had seemed as disinterested in the firm as she had been in resuming her studies.

So, why had she brought up Roxanne now? Of course, they needed to take care of the firm's matters. Kailash was working hard to consolidate its affairs. Once that was done, they could dissolve the company. And move forward with their lives. At least, that was how Kailash and he were seeing it.

Does she have something else in mind? She's overly emotional, was always prone to impulsiveness. Was this her way of giving direction to her grief; of finding closure?

He tried to calm himself down.

They could advance the wedding. If it made her happy, they could get married right now, before he left for Germany. Neena could join him there later, when her visa was processed. Meanwhile, she could resolve the matters of the firm with Kailash. It would keep her occupied and help her heal from the loss of her parents. Attending office would also make her realise how little any of them knew about the world of business, and how impossible it was for them to turn a sick, loss-making company around.

5

The preparations for the wedding were on in full swing. It would be a small ceremony, but he hoped it would give Neena the closure she needed so desperately.

The day finally dawned. Neena was radiant in her soft gold lehnga, delicately embroidered all over with maroon thread. The traditional Kashmiri headband and waistband from her mother's collection, family heirlooms, were perfect for her peachy pink complexion. Her light eyes were enhanced by the jewellery his mother had lovingly selected for her youngest daughter-in-law. The gold chain that dangled from the *dejhoor* reminded Kailash of Neena's mother's beauty.

Neena came down the stairs, as if emerging from a dream and went out into the lawns of her father's Victorian-style bungalow in Civil Lines, where the wedding rituals would take place. Sanjay was captivated by her beauty. He felt lucky to have found the woman and the professional opportunity of his dreams.

Wedding over, they went on a short but blissful trip to Mussoorie. By this time, Sanjay's immigration papers had been processed. But since Kamal had died intestate, the paperwork related to Roxanne Industries was complicated. Some assets and accounts had been in his name, while others had been in the name of the company. Neena's nomination as Kamal's legal heir was an essential step before they could initiate the closure of the firm. After a protracted process, finally, the paperwork was in order.

Neena, however, had other thoughts.

"You are deserting me. Why can't we stay here, and you take charge of the company?"

Sanjay tried to reason with her.

"Neena, that is not feasible. The firm has run up huge losses, and I really can't turn it around. I am a pharmacologist, not a businessman."

But her hysteria wouldn't listen.

"Neena, you know I have always wanted to do research. We will build our new life together in Germany. It is only a matter of a few months; then you can join me there."

"Roxanne is all that I have left of my parents. I will kill myself if you take it away from me!"

He was stunned.

Neena was not comprehending the reality of having to run a company they knew little about, in a field they knew nothing about. But she was grieving and in no condition to be left alone. Sanjay found himself in a quandary.

Thankfully, his request—by a few months—for deferment of his tenure was accepted by the university. That would give them time to deliver the existing orders at the firm, and for Neena to come around to his point of view.

For Sanjay, there was no option but to plunge headfirst into the affairs of the company, just as Kailash had done. A series of defaulted loans had spoilt the credibility of the firm. Kailash had worked hard to mobilise finances. Now they had to deliver on the final commitments made by Kamal Pandit. They tried to get Neena to come to office, but she was unable to concentrate on work, and would get nervous and excitable.

"Neena seems to have inherited more than her mother's beauty," Kailash casually mentioned one day, as Sanjay and he were working on inventories. Sanjay, who had only heard about her mother's mental illness in passing reference, was dumbfounded.

"Aren't you overreacting? She has been through so much. She must be feeling terribly alone."

He had quickly sidestepped the discussion, but often found himself remembering Kailash's words in the weeks that followed.

Sanjay had found a small house for Neena and himself in the plush South Delhi locality of Vasant Vihar. She had been reluctant to move there. "I want to be near my parents' memories."

"Neena, your parents will always be a part of you. Giving yourself some space will help you move on."

"How can you ask me to move on? Do you know how I feel?" she had shrieked. "You always want to take things away from me!"

He had given in. *It was only for a short while,* he told himself.

Kailash and he worked overtime to fulfil their orders.

Neena seemed less morose—almost happy—at times. He began to see glimpses of the gentle, kind and down-to-earth young woman he had fallen in love with, sometime ago.

Meanwhile, Kailash had identified a good opportunity to offload the factory. It would be the first step in closing down the company. But the very mention of this set Neena's teeth on edge. She flung a huge glass vase at Sanjay when he brought home the papers and had to be restrained physically.

"You are running away from me. You promised that you would manage Roxanne! So why do you want to sell the factory now?"

Leaving a sedated Neena in Kailash's care, Sanjay had travelled alone to Banaras, to his parents' home. The wedding had been rushed, and this was a trip his parents had been looking forward to. They had arranged for a ceremony to introduce Neena to their extended family—her new family. They had made elaborate arrangements for her welcome, only to be let down by her absence. Sanjay's parents' shock turned to concern on seeing his distress. They asked few questions, offered no criticism, and provided much support. His mother kept her disappointment to herself and went about pampering her son with his favourite red chilli pickle and mathris. His scholarly father tried to ignore his intuition that the present circumstances were just the tip of a deep iceberg that his youngest child was finding himself confronted by.

In the few days they spent together, they tried their best to give Sanjay some relief from his troubles. But Sanjay remained disturbed. He spent the evenings on the ghats of the Ganga. Even the synchronic sound of the conch shells, the rhythmic chants and the hundreds of brass lamps lit up against the sunset were not enough to calm his restless mind. His childhood friends, who visited him and invoked memories of their frequent swims in the river or the instances of bunking school to trek along the road to Ramnagar Fort, were also not able to get him to lighten up.

For Sanjay, the trip home, which he had planned with much anticipation, was a blur, and he went about the preparations for the ceremony mechanically. The hall decorated with flowers, the pandit reciting prayers, and the many guests blessing him, seemed to be distant happenings.

The shrill, screeching ring of the telephone in the hall brought him back to the moment.

He shouted into the phone, "Hello, hello!"

"Neena...hospital...wrist...blood...serious..." Kailash was sobbing into the phone.

There was no time for his mother to pack the traditional Banarasi sarees she had bought for Neena, or the kachoris that were a local specialty. The flight from Banaras to Bombay seemed to take longer than the flight to Germany that he would be forced to cancel very soon.

In the hospital, Neena's fair-complexioned face seemed ghost-like against the white pillows. He took in her heavily bandaged wrists and her sunken eyes. He could hardly recognise the sallow-faced woman who was staring blankly at the ceiling. Was this the person he had committed himself, his life, and his dreams to?

"She is sedated. She will recover."

He hoped she would. And that, he would stop feeling so detached from the woman he had courted, loved and married. Alongside this was another thought. If he felt so lost and overwhelmed, how would she be feeling? He must stand by her. And life would find its course again.

A week later, he brought her home. She was frail and easily fatigued.

It would be a long road to recovery. A road without signages for guidance, and only his instinct to give him direction.

One evening, as he helped Neena back into bed after their short walk together, he finally told her.

"I have declined the post-doctoral opportunity."

Her eyes lit up.

"Thank you. I knew you would come around."

"Neena, what do you want from our life?"

"You, me, and Roxanne."

He had expected this response. And had tried to prepare himself for it.

Right now, he needed Neena to step away from the melancholy. If it meant having to put his dream on hold and work at Roxanne instead, he would have to do that. Once Neena, and their life together, found more stability, he could explore other options. But, despite this realisation, he was unable to convince himself to continue living in what was his late father in-law's home. The roots of tradition ran deep in his family and his psyche: a man didn't live on in the home of his in-laws. He had to move with his wife into a separate dwelling.

A deal, the first of many he would strike in business, life and love, was struck. Neena agreed to move to the new home he had found for them. In return, she would transfer the firm's ownership to Sanjay; she *insisted* that he take charge of it. And there would be no more talk of selling it. In spite of his reluctance, Sanjay agreed. He just hoped that this change would help her finally get out of the deep, dark woods.

6

Neena immersed herself in setting up the house, and Sanjay, the company.

The firm had bitten off more than it could chew. The bitter taste would take a while to go away. Sanjay would put in long hours at work and return home to Neena. This was a new phase in their relationship, calm and reassuring. He would share the developments at the factory with her, and she would listen intently. And then, she would tell him about her painting, a passion she had revived recently, and which was helping some of her sadness found release. The moments they spent together reminded him of the simple times of their college life. It was a new rhythm, a tentative one. But an encouraging one, nonetheless—except for the times when Neena would turn depressive.

It had been a few weeks after this that Mahima had walked into Roxanne. By then, production and distribution had shown the results of Sanjay and Kailash's efforts. The number-crunching remained as complex as ever, though, and Sanjay needed an accountant to handle that task. He had been preoccupied and brief with Mahima that first day, not really expecting her to show up for the job. But she had.

He had been surprised, not at her lack of experience, but by the self-assured manner in which she had conducted herself. The few other candidates he had interviewed hadn't had any work experience, either. But they had been younger, somewhat flippant and not earnest. In Mahima, he had seen a quiet confidence and maturity that were unusual for her age.

7

Mahima had grown up in Calcutta, in one of the many families of Burra Bazaar. Her Marwari home was traditional but not backward. Between her grandparents, uncles and cousins, the family traded in sugar, sarees and jute. In the five-generational joint family, her parents were sandwiched in the middle. The third of five brothers, her father Raunak took care of a saree shop. His wife Anju was an important part of the buzzing family hive of older and younger women and children. Known for her austerity and pragmatism, she found herself straddled with responsibilities beyond just looking after her only child.

Mahima had enjoyed growing up in the large home with cramped rooms teeming with aunts, uncles and cousins of all ages. She revelled in the recognition she found in the girls' school she attended. Her intellect and interest in academics singled her out from the many other students. She enjoyed the undivided attention of her teachers when they realised her intuitive grasp of studies, especially mathematics.

Many boys and girls of their community married young. That would have been Mahima's fate too, if it hadn't been for the illness of her step-grandmother, which kept her mother and the other elders preoccupied. Her father encouraged her to make use of the opportunity to attend college and help him at the shop

Completing school, she had joined the Intermediate CA course. Her days at college gave her a window to life beyond Burra Bazaar, which had earlier seemed a complete—if chaotic—world in itself. She found the window to be an eye-opener.

Weddings in their community were as much about suitable trade and business alliances as about a match between man and woman. In that sense, the Mathur family in Jodhpur was a perfect match for theirs. Mahima's grandfather believed that the Mathurs' offices and contacts in Rajasthan would be helpful in expanding their sugar trade, and a meeting was arranged.

Pawan's mother had dominated the conversation. "Calcutta is such a fascinating place, bhai sahib! So different from our tiny village. My son is the first one from our family to study engineering. He wants a wife who is educated."

His father, who weighed half as much as his mother and spoke barely a quarter of what she did, hadn't said anything much.

"Don't worry, behen ji. Mahima was interested in studies and has attended college. And, coming from a large family, she will adjust well to your household."

"No, Pawan wants to work in some foreign company, like his friends from IIT. After all, the label of IIT will get him a good job in Delhi or Bombay."

Mahima and Pawan had been given the perfunctory five minutes alone with each other.

"I have a job offer in Delhi. I have never liked living in a large family. I just want it to be you and me," he said.

Typical of events in their community, but contrary to their family's usual lifestyle, the wedding had been an elaborate affair. Tall and fair, Pawan had opted for a formal suit instead of the traditional sherwani. Mahima's aunt had selected identical wedding lehengas for her and her cousin, who was to get married a few months later. Pawan had mocked the traditional style for weeks after the wedding.

"You must understand that I want a modern life. Not old-fashioned, like the one you have seen. City life is what the future is."

The wedding in Calcutta had been followed by a reception in Pawan's village near Jodhpur. The wedding party had travelled to Rajasthan by train. Segregated by gender, they had occupied four coaches of the train, and the festivities had continued throughout their journey. For Mahima, the brief stay with Pawan's family was a rustic version of her life in Calcutta.

Pawan and she could be alone only when the train chugged out from Jodhpur railway station. This journey to Delhi, where Pawan had recently taken up a job, had been short. But it had seemed interminable. Pawan, who everyone had told her was the silent type, had turned out to be anything but. He had been irritable, too. And, demanding.

"Why didn't you check the berths allotted to us?"

The side berths were smaller, and a little less comfortable, than the ones in the main bays of the coach.

"Pawan, *you* went to get the tickets."

"But you should have checked them, too."

And so on. The ordeal continued the next morning, when the train reached Delhi. "Decide the rates with the coolie properly. They always try and cheat. It is all your luggage, after all."

She liked the buzz of excitement that Delhi had, though the sounds and the crowds would take some getting used to. Their new home in Old Rajinder Nagar was waiting for her. The lanes leading from the busy main road into the rows of houses, whose numbering she would never understand, were as small as the ones in Burra Bazaar. And more cluttered, if that was possible. There was a sense of urgency in this city that, she thought, she would never be able to understand or identify with.

She began setting up the kitchen and the home with the fixed allowance Pawan gave her. She was keen to start the new life he wanted—with just the two of them. But she didn't know that this feeling would last only a short while.

One day, feeling unwell and fatigued, she had convinced Pawan to take her to a doctor. The news of her pregnancy had left her anxious. And Pawan's indifference had intensified that feeling.

"This is unexpected."

Weren't you the one who had told me not to use birth control? she thought.

The pregnancy had not been difficult after the initial months. But the isolation had been tough on her. Being alone at home all day was new for her. She began to explore the markets and other places around their home.

"Why were you away when I returned?"

"I had gone to Karol Bagh to buy bedsheets. Got late."

"The other day too, you went out."

"It is boring to be indoors all day, with nothing to do."

"Try and cook something new. And you must be more careful with money. You spend too much."

He would return home in the evening to the tea and snacks she kept ready for him. The sounds of the television—that she had brought as part of her dowry—which filled the room in the evening were scant compensation for the perpetual activity and conversation that used to take place in the square courtyard of her Calcutta home.

"Pawan, *tai* had called, asking me when I will go to Calcutta for the delivery."

"Why would you go to Calcutta?"

"It is a tradition that the baby should be born at the mother's parents' home."

"Mahima, I don't believe in all this. We are an educated, modern couple. We can surely manage our lives ourselves. Besides, you need to take care of the house here!"

In the end, they had decided that she would deliver the baby in Delhi, and her mother and *tai* would stay with them for some time to help her with the new-born. Pavan had known that her mother and *tai* were old-fashioned enough to not stay in his house for more than a few days. And he had been right. Those days had passed very quickly.

By the time Piyu was 40 days old, Mahima had finally convinced Pawan to travel with her to Calcutta. Being back home did give her the physical rest she needed, but it also made her feel a relaxation that was beyond that of the body. She felt a calmness she had almost forgotten existed.

"I can't stay here for long. It is not tradition. Besides, I only have so much leave."

Ha! So you believe in customs and traditions only when it is convenient for you? she'd wondered.

Her mother and *tai* had implored Pawan, "Let Mahima and Piyu stay here for a few weeks."

"You can keep Piyu for a few months if you want. That will give Mahima time to get the Delhi house in order," he had replied.

Everyone had assumed he was joking and had laughed. But Mahima had been stunned. Because she knew he was dead serious. Pawan had been demanding during her pregnancy, be it for his meals or having the home run to his liking. But in the days just after Piyu's birth, he had become unreasonable. The modernity he spoke of was a myth. Or, something he embraced only at his convenience. If it hadn't been for Gayatri aunty, who lived in the house below theirs in Delhi, she wouldn't have been able to manage with her baby at all.

She had quickly changed the topic. "Pawan is joking, *tai*. We will come back soon. Anyway, life is so fast-paced in Delhi that we hardly realise where time goes."

"Yes, modern big-city life is like that," Pawan had added.

The journey back to Delhi had been momentous, and not just because Pawan had agreed to travel by air. Holding Piyu close to her at the airport, getting ready to board the flight, she had been struck by a realisation. She had earlier thought she was missing her family. But now, she knew she had been wrong. She was actually missing *herself!* The Mahima who enjoyed reading the newspaper, discussing the news with her father, and participating in family decisions found herself imprisoned with Pawan and stonewalled by him all the time. The confidence that the simple girl from Calcutta had always possessed had gradually eroded in the past year. The joy she had found in matching her bangles, trying out new styles for her long hair and shopping for a variety of textiles and weaves had been forgotten. She was losing sight of the lively, intelligent and sharp young woman she had always been.

Returning home to Delhi came with more restrictions and rules for her.

"Mahima, now our expenses will go up. You must be more careful!"

While she had had no expectations that he would help her manage Piyu, she hadn't been prepared for his unreasonable behaviour. He was almost jealous of the time she gave to Piyu.

"Mahima, I didn't get any sleep last night. How can I be expected to work if things go on like this? There will be problems at the office."

So she had taken to sleeping in the small living room next to the kitchen, leaving the bedroom to Pawan.

"Mahima, my trousers aren't ironed!"

"Food has to be ready on time. Adjust Piyu's sleeping schedule accordingly."

She could handle the chores. But the fact that he seemed to treat her as just an appendage of himself was difficult to accept.

Pawan loved Piyu, but only as long as he didn't have to change his routine or preferences for her. That was how he was with Mahima, too. She now noticed how his large family in Jodhpur was vastly different from her close-knit and connected one in Calcutta. And Pawan was hardly involved in his family's matters. He wasn't close to even his parents!

As Piyu grew, Mahima had found herself spending more and more of the day at Gayatri aunty's house. The elderly woman, grieving the husband she had lost a few months ago, had found this as much a respite from loneliness as Mahima did.

Also, Mahima had begun to plan for Piyu's education.

"I will send her to the best school in Delhi. A co-ed modern school," she told Pawan one evening.

His retort had been quick, and along predictable lines. "But we must save money."

Pawan, the IIT graduate with a corporate job, found it very difficult to spend money on anyone other than himself.

"Gayatri aunty, it is so boring to always stay at home and look after a baby."

"Beti, it is always boring to do something that doesn't fulfil you. Why don't you take up a job?"

"How can I, aunty? Piyu is little. And I have to look after the house, too."

"The house, beti, is something that starts looking after itself when it has to. Likewise, the menfolk," the elderly lady had quietly advised her.

"You look for a job. I will look after Piyu."

The affection between Gayatri aunty and little Piyu was mutual. And one that the child would forever be grateful for.

Mahima had begun to pore over the classifieds in the newspaper. She had anticipated resistance from Pawan. His remarks were different on each day. But the essence and the snideness were the same every day.

"I don't think your protected environment has equipped you to work in Delhi."

"You have no experience. Offices in Delhi are not like your family's saree shops. They need people with a professional background."

"You haven't even cleared the final level of CA. You won't stand a chance."

Just going out for a job interview, and the break it had given her from the stifling atmosphere at home, felt like a gush of oxygen. These short reprieves made his snide remarks tolerable or, at least, gave her the restraint to ignore them.

Even after she joined Roxanne, she had expected it to be only a brief stint. Pawan had been uncooperative, always deriding her decision.

"I don't think we can afford a new refrigerator. Besides, fresh food is best for Piyu."

"Must be a failed company, if they are recruiting someone like you."

"Piyu will be neglected. Is this how you were brought up?"

Yet, Mahima had persisted. It had been difficult, especially handling the guilt regarding Piyu that Pavan kept unleashing on her. But the need to get away from the oppressive environment, even if for just a few hours, was overwhelming. As she had expected, the work was a distraction for her fatigued mind. Being away from home, free from Pawan's expectations and demands, was soothing for her frayed nerves.

8

When she had joined the company, the finances had been in a state of shambles. None of the ledgers were in order, and the firm was in heavy debt. She had her work cut out, and quickly got used to working in the sparse office, with the pedestal fan making her an unlikely comrade for her silent boss.

She was struck by Sanjay's dedication to his work and the infinite patience he possessed. It was a rare occasion when he would show anger or frustration. His commitment was what kept the other employees motivated. But the permanent furrow on his forehead and the fatigue in his eyes were reminders that he was suppressing pain and sorrow.

His tenderness and concern for her were not lost on her. Their silent companionship gave her the confidence to not waver from her decision to continue her job even in the face of Pawan's opposition. On days when Pawan would be overly argumentative and she would reach office a little late, Sanjay would take her fluster in his stride and allow her to settle down before handing her the work files. And, if she was disturbed about having to leave a crying Piyu behind, he would sense that something was wrong and ask her if she wanted time off to go to the canteen. He never asked her for answers and explanations. It was as if he knew that she was in a state more fragile than she herself realised.

She immersed herself in the work and became comfortable with him and their silence. They hardly spoke, except for brief discussions about the firm's accounts.

For Sanjay, though, it was different. He had been totally caught up in work when she had joined, but he had noticed her immediately. Her confidence in her work was reflected in her notes and summaries that she began drawing up. But there was also something about her that intrigued him. It wasn't just her demure self, dressed in a simple cotton saree or salwar kameez, her long hair tied in a tight plait, sitting at her desk, nibbling at her pencil or toying nervously with the mangal sutra she wore.

It was her reserve and her stoic silence. They resonated with him. Without being offensive or rude, she would just be distant. She was someone who had got used to putting away her feelings and emotions in boxes and burying them deep within, so she didn't have to confront them. What might be interpreted by most people as her calmness had much turbulence hidden beneath it. His heart recognised it, correctly, as pain. The reluctant owner of Roxanne Industries found himself drawn to his taciturn new employee.

9

The office acquired more chairs and a filing cabinet. A desert cooler, that left a musty smell even after it was switched off, replaced the pedestal fan. Kailash recruited Arjun, who went on to become one of their most dedicated employees. An aluminium partition with a frosted glass door was constructed to make a cubicle for Sanjay. His intense discussion with bankers or companies wouldn't distract the others from their work anymore, but Mahima was usually privy to these animated conversations.

She had managed to organise all the ledgers and account books. A series of loan defaults had affected the company's credibility. Her first proposal was to settle those, even if it meant taking new orders to generate income. Sanjay had dismissed the ambitious plan as the overconfidence of the inexperienced. But Kailash, discerning and perceptive as ever, commented, "Her ideas have potential. And she has the confidence to take them through."

Brainstorming sessions to devise strategies to stay afloat replaced the silent 11 am cups of tea. In the unpredictable monsoons, Sanjay and Mahima would stop at the tea stall on the ground floor of their building and have a double chai as they watched the rain form puddles, then fill the potholes and finally, the roads. Soon, it felt like they had been doing this forever.

For Mahima, work was an escape—a respite—from her unhappiness. The listlessness she carried from home disappeared when she entered the office. The discussions left her enthused, and Sanjay's company made her feel light. Discussing the company's finances with him gave her a chance to relive the moments she had spent in her father's saree shop in the small by-lanes of old Calcutta. She had spent her evenings there, supervising the staff and helping clients select the choicest of bargains. And, as night fell, they would close the accounts for the day, with the shutter half down. She would separate the currency notes of different denominations and mark the credit purchases in red across the respective customer's names.

She was now organising Roxanne's finances in the same meticulous manner. Immersed in her work, she began to see flashes of the person she used to be; not the person she was always trying to be at home, worrying about upsetting Pawan or provoking his rage in any way. In the evening, like the handbag she slung on her shoulder, the heaviness would descend on her. She would return home to tread softly on the eggshells of Pawan's hostility and aggression.

After she would leave the office, Sanjay would think about the day gone by. Sometimes, he would walk her to the bus stop, using the opportunity to get a smoke. He would observe her fidgeting with her plait or her dupatta as she waited for the bus—and her nervousness when the bus, already running late, ambled towards them. Why was the girl who was a whiz with numbers, and self-assured and confident in the office, suddenly a bundle of nerves?

Despite the hours they spent at work together, she never spoke about herself. It was days after having coffee together for the first time that she told him that she had never tasted coffee before. And it was only when she asked for a day off for Piyu's school admission that he saw her eyes sparkle.

When she left in the evening, she would leave her desk clear of even a single pen or a sheet of paper. She never used the extra chair in office to hang her handbag; she'd always hang in on her chair. She had certainly got used to taking up the least possible space, in her physical presence and in conversation. *How, and when, did she become so used to being invisible?* Sanjay would wonder. The pain she was suppressing in herself found resonance with the hurt he carried in his heart.

She seemed fragile, and a part of him would want to reach out and touch her; hold her burdens for just a few moments. He would wonder at her withdrawn nature, wishing he could ask her what all she was holding back. Given the easy camaraderie that had developed between them and the time they spent together, he could have asked. But he never did. He knew that it could be the undoing of this resolve, and of the front, that she carefully maintained. How could he not know this? He had been there, too. He was beginning to feel drawn to her sorrows and loneliness because that was what his heart carried, too. But, for now, he had to hold back the tenderness he could feel welling up in him whenever she was close to him. These were feelings best avoided. He would try not to think of anything other than the sheets and statements she would bring him. At the same time, he would wait for their daily walk to the coffee house, and for her to return to his desk after lunch. He would be aware of her presence every moment of the day.

But she seemed unaware of all this. *This strange comfort zone is for the best,* he reminded himself.

Work, and life, continued.

10

The arid warmth from the conduction heater filled the room. The darkness and chill of a North Indian winter would descend even before afternoon could give way to evening.

A crucial meeting with bank officials was scheduled for the coming week. Mahima had made the changes they had discussed and brought him the proposal for the meeting.

"Can we discuss this briefly?" he asked her. She hesitated.

"Sorry, I didn't realise you were leaving. We can do this tomorrow."

"No, no, it's okay. I think we should discuss it now. There are still some loopholes."

She leaned across the table, explaining the figures that didn't add up. He quickly noted down the points she had listed to work on them through the night. As she finished, the edginess returned. It made him want to reach out to her; to touch her and calm her.

"Let me walk you to the bus stop."

They walked past the hawkers with roasted peanuts and waited for the bus in the chilly wind. She pulled her cardigan close to her chest and buttoned it up.

He surprised himself by reaching for her hand. He would immediately have withdrawn it if she hadn't clasped it back. They stood hand in hand, wordlessly waiting for the bus to arrive. When it did, she held his hand just a little bit longer and then boarded it. Even after the bus was out of sight, he could feel her hand trembling in his. He returned to the office and tried to focus on the papers she had left on his table. But he was distracted by the feelings that had gushed through him when he had squeezed her fingers in his, and by the unspoken closeness he could feel developing between both of them. He found himself crying silently; tears of kinship that pain brought.

In the bus, Mahima should have been anxious. Pawan would be angry about her coming home late. Instead, she looked down at her palms. And felt the warmth of reassurance that holding Sanjay's hands, even for just those few minutes, had given her.

Both were too busy the next few days to dwell upon how holding hands had brought solace to a troubled friend—and themselves. The preparations for the meeting and the series of presentations kept them occupied and tense.

They were successful in their applications for new loan schemes. Roxanne Industries, which had become Roxanne Pharmaceuticals, was back in business, and could even look forward to growing. The 40 employees in the factory were excited about the mechanisation of the setup. Usually a prudent spender, Sanjay indulged in a large neon sign and put it up outside the office building. Finally, he felt he could announce the company's presence to the world.

He knew he wouldn't have been able to pull off this turnaround without Mahima's hard work and Kailash's encouragement. Or the faith his staff had placed in him. They would celebrate, and grow, together.

Meanwhile, Neena's bouts of hysteria and her wild mood swings had been diagnosed as bipolar disorder. Coping with her mood shifts and her fear of abandonment was not easy. He truly cherished the moments when she was her natural self: caring, compassionate and communicative. But those moments were few, and usually not when he needed them. It was as if the gentle, soft-spoken woman he had fallen in love with was now trapped in this tangled web of anger, sadness and mania. Despite the fact that Neena was always hovering around him, he had started feeling alone. The struggles and successes of the firm he had taken over for her would get lost in her chatter about painting the nursery or about her latest artwork. His thoughts never found release at home. Helplessness and guilt had become his companions, and Neena's unpredictability made him feel increasingly lonely. He was relieved when she accepted the diagnosis of her condition and began taking her medication.

He hoped this would be the start of a better chapter for them. He had dedicated himself to the company so that Neena would feel more secure and be able to find happiness. And now, perhaps, she could attend office and finally be a part of the company. Reviving her career might be the distraction she needed from her longing for a baby. A longing that seemed unlikely to be fulfilled.

"I am happy at home, Sanjay. You go." Neena's refusal shocked him.

He had planned this evening so enthusiastically! How could she not be a part of the celebrations?

"It is *your* company, Neena. I was hoping you will start visiting the office now."

"No, I don't want to join office. I will stay at home."

"But at least today, Neena, you must come. It is a very important day for us."

"Yes, Sanjay, it is. And, I am glad for you. Hope you have a good evening."

It was like a punch in his gut. Neena wanted Roxanne to be a part of her life but did not want to be an active participant in it. Just like her relationship with Sanjay.

It isn't her; it is the disease, he told himself. But it didn't make things better.

That evening, as he drove to the *havan* ceremony at the factory, the intense loneliness seemed to pierce his heart. He tried to shake the mood away. The benevolent smile of Lord Ganesha and the rituals of the pooja would ordinarily have soothed him. But that evening, the flames rising from the *havan kund* only managed to sear his face. As the priest chanted his mantras, Sanjay pleaded with the deity to extend his blessings to the marriage he had begun to resent. He prayed for forgiveness for being unable to create for Neena and himself the happiness that the marriage should have brought.

Despite his preoccupations, he was acutely aware of Mahima's absence at the function. It was unlike her to miss such a significant occasion. She had been enthusiastic about the plans for the *havan* and the first Family Day celebrations of Roxanne. The prize distribution, employee awards and mementos had all been her ideas.

Fairy lights on trees, bright canopies, and the stage with coloured tube lights made for a festive ambience. It was a beautiful evening, and everyone enjoyed the performances and the food. Having to fulfil his father in-law's dream had been a compulsion for Sanjay, but now, the company had begun to feel like family.

He stepped out of the main hall into the reception for a smoke. That's when he saw her.

Her hair was tied in a tight bun and adorned with flowers. He suddenly wished he was close enough to smell them. The palla of her translucent Chanderi saree was draped perfectly over her arm. Silver jhumkas swung gently below her ears, and matching bangles clinked at her wrists. Mahima looked beautiful.

Before he could realise that her eyes were puffy, he saw Pawan walking a few steps behind her. She waited for Pawan to catch up with her. It wasn't just her looks that had captured Sanjay's attention. It was her nervousness. For the rest of the evening, he would be acutely aware of it. The desire to hold her close was compelling.

He noted her taut face and hesitant replies when he welcomed them.

"You didn't bring your daughter?"

"No, she was tired."

After brief, formal introductions with Pawan, Sanjay busied himself in mingling with the other guests. Mahima and Pawan remained close to each other all evening, hardly interacting with the others. Yet, it didn't seem like they were together. She was edgy, not even helping herself to the cold drink without first checking on Pawan. But Pawan was dismissive of her efforts to make him comfortable or to start a conversation. From his corner near the buffet table, Sanjay was wondering about them. The tense woman trying to appease her husband over everything was a far cry from the confident accountant who drafted proposals for lakhs of rupees and presented them to bankers.

The merriment of the evening's cultural program touched everyone. He had wanted Neena to give away the prizes for the musical program and encourage the staff. But, in her absence, he attended to the task himself. He handed the toys packed in shiny paper to the children who came up to the stage. In the distance, he noted Pawan storming off, and Mahima trailing behind him, her dinner remaining unfinished on the plate she had hastily abandoned.

Party over, he felt the loneliness return. Before going home, he drove past the office. From the fourth floor, the blue of the neon sign fell onto the road below, giving it an incandescent hue. He could feel its warmth. The warmth of having succeeded in the face of phenomenal challenges. He tried to ignore the shadows that formed just outside the spill of the blue light, and headed home.

Back home, he checked the pillbox to confirm that Neena had taken her medications, but his thoughts were of Mahima. He was wondering what it was that she carried in her heart, and if he could lessen her burden in any way. *No,* he told himself. *Like me, she will have to deal with it herself. This is how it is, and that is how it must continue to be.*

And it did.

Until the day everything about their life changed.

11

The change from Roxanne Industries to Roxanne Pharmaceuticals was beyond semantics. The hard work Kailash had put in even before Sanjay had joined the firm, and Som's efforts in building the factory township—where he now lived—had borne fruit. Sanjay's stewardship and his persistence were obvious to everyone, as were Mahima's confidence and vision. This new phase saw a shift in their management structure and future projections, something they had all worked hard for.

They were neck-deep in work. Every day. Every week. There was such a lot to be done.

The tenders for new machines had been opened. Mahima had drawn up comparisons of the tenders.

"It's been a long day."

She placed the four-page sheaf on his table, with her observations detailed in the margins.

"Yes, you are running late. You should be getting home now."

"I know, but we should complete this today."

She sank into the chair opposite him, removed her slippers and folded her legs under her, like she always did when she sat there.

Sanjay called for chai. They worked in silence, he poring over the charts and she double-checking the brochures of the bidding companies. The silence was interrupted by the phone ringing.

"It's for you," he said and passed her the receiver.

Her arm briefly brushed against his as she took it. "Yes, I will take time."

The voice at the other end was muffled, but the tone was definitely unpleasant. He saw her try to control her tears. As if reading his mind, she turned to face away from him as she waited to get a word in.

"I told you this is a busy week. There is dal in the fridge. And Reshma will make chapatis."

Sanjay knew the line was dead even before she said, "Yes, bye, don't worry," and pretended to end the call on a pleasant note.

A few seconds later, she returned to the brochures and the chai that had arrived. The few seconds were not enough to hide her trembling and her attempt to control her tears. He silently passed her the cup of tea and moved to the bamboo sofa by the bay window. She followed him there, gingerly dipped a biscuit into the hot tea and scooped it into her mouth. She fixed a few loose strands of hair and tucked them into her plait as she waited for the steaming brew to cool down. Her nervousness was back.

One stubborn strand of hair simply wouldn't stay put. It swung from her forehead, almost dipping into the teacup.

Sanjay extended his hand and tucked it behind her ear. His hand lingered on her face for the briefest moment before he took her hand in his and clasped it ever so tightly. She, in turn, pressed his hand deep and hard, as if it were giving her some form of strength.

They sat there like that, the papers forgotten, and the tea ignored. This was a different silence, a mix of stillness and anticipation. They would never know who came closer first. He held her close to him, gently caressing her forehead. She began to sob. He sat still, lest the slightest movement make her conscious and compel her to move away. They let her tears fall. A few moments later, he gently began wiping them away. He didn't remove his hands from her face. He let some of the tears fall on his palms, mixing with her smudged kajal that had transferred to his fingers. When the sobbing subsided, he kissed her on the head, then the forehead. They sat there, holding each other close. He was aware of softness: of her skin at her waist, under the saree she was wearing, of her hair that barely managed to separate his face from hers, and of her hands in his. She felt the comfort of his arms and the warmth of his breath on her face.

Those few moments, with her head resting against his chest, and the light bulb flickering with the fluctuation in voltage, seemed like hours. Suddenly aware of her surroundings, she stiffened. He removed his arms from her shoulders. She took the handkerchief he offered her and wiped her eyes. They stood up together. She fumbled for her slippers and adjusted her saree. Then, he kissed her. All over her face and on the lips. It was as if their parched mouths had been waiting to find each other's tongues for ages. Finally, they disentangled themselves from their embrace and looked at each other silently.

"Let me drop you home."

"No, it's okay. I will take the bus."

"Please, Mahima, I won't feel comfortable knowing that you haven't reached home."

She waited at the door.

They walked to his car. And even before he revved up the engine, he reached for her hand again. She clasped it. After what seemed like a lifetime, he started the car, stealing sideways glances at her and holding her hand whenever he didn't need to switch gears. Her face was expressionless as she looked out of the window; a contrast to the intensity with which she held his hand.

He knew her address (having snuck a look at her resume many days ago). But, as he approached the busy Shankar Road, he slowed, waiting for her to guide him.

"You can stop here. My house is just behind this sweetshop."

He waited and kept watching her walk into the lane, until the cars behind him began to honk. He wondered if he should return to office or go home. Home seemed to be another universe. He returned to office. There he sat at her desk, feeling her hand in his, and her presence near him.

She crossed the sweetshop bustling with activity. Her pace quickened as she passed the boutiques that stitched ladies' clothes; they had downed their shutters more than an hour ago. She knew Pawan would be angry. Yet, she paused at their second-floor landing before ringing the bell. Looking down at her palms, she could feel Sanjay's short, stubby fingers caress her slender ones as he had bent to kiss her.

The silence at home was stifling. Pawan was sulking, as usual. The food was untouched. Reshma handed her a glass of water. "Piyu betu had her food."

Mahima pushed Sanjay's kiss to the back of her mind, nodded gratefully at Reshma and went to meet Piyu, who was packing her school bag for the next day. Later, when the child had slept, Pawan vented his anger on Mahima.

"You are neglecting Piyu and the house!"

"I told you there was important work. I had told Reshma what to prepare."

"These are *your* responsibilities, not Reshma's. Too much ambition will not get you anywhere."

She knew that replying, or even trying to explain, would only fuel his anger further. It was strange how choosing not to engage could also be so exhausting. There was so much about their relationship that she could never expect anyone to understand.

"Reshma is becoming too arrogant. You should look for a replacement."

Of course, you would suggest such a thing, she thought. It was Reshma's presence that made it possible for her to go to work without having to worry about Piyu. And Pavan couldn't stand that.

It had been some time ago that Reshma had turned up at her doorstep, holding her belongings wrapped in a sheet and hiding her bruises under a scarf. It had been a stroke of luck that Pawan had been away from Delhi at that time. By the time he returned, the petite girl had made herself indispensable to the household. Saying that having Reshma around was a frivolous expense was something he often did, but Mahima had stuck to her decision of keeping her. The first few years after Piyu had been born, Gayatri aunty had looked after her. But then, she had begun to travel often to be with her children and grandchildren. Day-care options were few and far between, and Reshma had been just what Mahima had needed.

Pawan's response was something she had expected. Usually, on days that ended like this, she would not be able to sleep without bouts of quiet sobbing. But today, she tossed and turned restlessly as she recalled the feelings that kissing Sanjay had evoked in her. She also recalled the tenderness in his caress, and how he had removed the pen from his shirt pocket when he had realised it would hurt her forehead. It was this ocean of kindness in him that had allowed her to unburden herself without the need for words or explanations.

Elsewhere, Sanjay recalled her slim frame next to him and her hand in his hand, and wondered at the depths of sorrow she was carrying within her.

The next morning, Pawan made no mention of the argument or his unreasonableness. He simply sauntered into the kitchen, where she was packing lunch for all of them along with Reshma.

"Piyu and I were wondering if we could drop you off at office on the way to school. Then you will be able to finish work in time. You need to manage time and your responsibilities better."

Piyu was excited about the new car. But for Mahima, it meant that the money he gave her for household expenses had reduced, and she had to dip into her income for the things she wanted to indulge her daughter with.

Seeing Piyu's excited smile, she gave in and slid into the back seat of the car a little later.

As she got off at her office building, she placed a tender kiss on Piyu's forehead and said, "Bye! Enjoy school!"

Piyu and Pawan waved back. To onlookers, they must have appeared to be a typical, happy, upwardly mobile middle-class family.

In office, without stopping at her desk, she had gone to Sanjay's cubicle. She waited for him to finish the call he was on.

"Hi! Do you want me to go over the applications one last time?"

"Just this clause, which I have marked with a pencil."

She didn't reach for the papers. Instead, she went across to his side of the table and bent down to read the part he was referring to. He was aware of her brushing against him, her dupatta falling gently over his thigh. And the quickening of his heartbeat. She was aware of a need to be close to him, to savour the calmness he always brought her. The spontaneity they felt with each other was strong. It was the start of a bond that defied definitions and would continue to do so.

12

They desperately looked forward to coming to work every day. Being close to each other, holding hands, the occasional hug and finding laughter unexpectedly in routine things meant that the day flew before they knew it.

Sanjay was aware of the yearning he felt for her and tried hard to control it. He was sure that the attraction was mutual. At the same time, he wondered whether she herself was aware and prepared for the turmoil she carried within herself.

He waited.

They began to speak of things they were enmeshed in. An emotionally unavailable husband, snuffed dreams of a bright career; her isolation, his helplessness; their pain and loneliness. There was space to share everything; an opportunity to feel each emotion without fear, guilt or judgement. And, of course, they spoke about Sanjay's passion for research.

"How different is drug research from the work we are doing?"

"Totally different, Mahima. We are only making the molecules and components that others have developed. Drug research involves *core* research, discovering and developing new drugs from scratch." Being able to speak about the carbon, hydrogen and oxygen molecules heartened Sanjay. Mahima didn't end those discussions abruptly or brush away his interests as a 'fancy that he was hanging onto'. She told him how her father had wanted her to complete her Chartered Accountancy course but Pawan's family had insisted on an early wedding.

They discovered a common interest in Hindi film songs and spent hours discussing their favourite Lata, Kishore, and Rafi melodies. He told her how he had stopped listening to them at home because Neena preferred classical music. And she told him how Pawan got enraged whenever she hummed along the songs playing on the cassette player.

They continued to draw strength from sharing their dreams, vulnerabilities and sorrows.

13

Neena had finally conceived. Her mood swings during early pregnancy had given way to extreme fatigue. Yet, she was looking healthier than she had in the last few years. He would return home to find her poring over a book of baby names or weaving crochet blankets for the baby—moments he savoured. Hearing her ask about his day was to recognise her attentiveness towards him all over again. He allowed himself the sliver of hope that these moments brought.

But it seemed that her dream of having a family was to remain just that. A dream.

The miscarriage coincided with the establishment of Roxanne's new factory in Sita Nagar.

He felt her pain. He could understand her grief, even her anger; but not the blame she inflicted on him.

Her medication for bipolar disorder had been stopped during her pregnancy; it seemed her mental illness was taking the shape of mania now. It alarmed him.

"I bet you are happy now. You never wanted the baby!" She hurled a book at him one day.

From time to time, she'd say, "All you ever think about is Roxanne!"

He was too numb to comment on the irony of her outrage. Devoting himself to the company was something he had done for *her*. At *her* behest.

The inauguration of the new factory also coincided with Pawan's resignation from his job. Mahima had assumed that his talk about quitting was a passing fancy. Pawan's rise in his career had been meteoric, and he would not have been short of opportunities—in his present company or elsewhere. He, though, wanted to use his sales expertise for the benefit of the small spices-and-condiments business his family ran in Jodhpur. Mahima was sure that the entrepreneurial bug was a consequence of her successful career, especially since she had been nominated as a director of the company recently.

"Let's move back to Jodhpur."

"Pawan, you always said that life in a big city is good for your career. And for Piyu's education, too. That's what you wanted."

"Yes, it is for Piyu that I am going into business. I can earn a lot more this way."

Her financial and emotional independence hadn't gone down well with him. She saw his decision for what it was—an opportunity for him to control her. An effort to wrest away from her the identity she had formed and nurtured in the last few years.

"But Piyu has settled down well in school. And I have my work, too."

"Your job is not the only thing in the world. You have a responsibility towards me, too. And to Piyu. You can look for a job there later."

"We are at a crucial phase of the company's growth, Pawan." Roxanne Pharmaceuticals had applied for listing on the Bombay Stock Exchange.

"It's just a job, Mahima. You are doing it only to occupy your time and prove that you can work."

The pattern was familiar. Their conversations would escalate into confrontations, which would then crash into a heavy, toxic silence.

14

The documentation necessary for listing on the stock exchange was complicated and tiresome. Listing was an ambitious target for a firm that was just a few years out of insolvency. But it was Mahima and Sanjay's hard work and vision that made it possible to consider new vistas.

"So these forms need to be submitted separately? Let me make a note of that. I may forget it."

"Let me take you through these again. Don't worry."

He wished she would be attending the meetings with him in Bombay. She was a natural with this stuff. The young girl who had spent her spare time in her father's shop and aced math exams had good business acumen.

"I wish Kailash uncle was well enough to travel with you to Bombay," she said as she took his hand in hers at the coffee shop. They had their favourite table, almost completely hidden by the large water cooler.

"Will you come with me?" he fumbled. "I mean, for the meetings." And after a brief pause, he added, "But it's okay. I understand."

She kept quiet. They sipped their coffee in silence.

A few days later, as she was punching some sheets into a folder, she thought, "Maybe I *should* travel to Bombay for these meetings, after all."

"Are you sure?" Sanjay asked her when she told him this.

"Yes, I want to be there."

Pawan had set up an office in the Jhandewalan area of Delhi. He divided his time between Delhi and Jodhpur.

He had invested heavily in his new enterprise, a risk she had advised him against.

"Why do you have to go to Bombay? You are neglecting Piyu. Besides, I will be going to Jodhpur. You need to oversee my packing also."

"It's only for a few days. I have worked so hard for this. This is a dream project. Reshma will look after Piyu."

"You shouldn't be having dreams that don't include your family."

Sanjay had travelled ahead and was at the Bombay railway station to receive her. Her pale blue kurta and churidar were uncreased after the night journey—like her face, on which her troubles never showed.

"Have you been to Bombay before?"

"No."

The city whizzed past as they took a taxi to their hotel. The city made no pretence of hiding the shanties and slums. The air conditioning of the taxi wasn't enough to prevent the sweat from moistening her back.

Alighting at the hotel, Sanjay checked her in.

She walked behind him along the carpeted corridor, until he stopped and turned the key into the door to one of the rooms.

"See you later. I am in 306, if you need anything."

He had travelled to Bombay a number of times already in connection with the listing. In the last few weeks, he had begun to feel at home in these hotel corridors and in his room. They were a respite from the volatile atmosphere of home. Here, he felt free for a few days, before returning to the well-done-up bungalow that was, nevertheless, a cage.

She entered her room and shut the door. This was the first time she was in a hotel without any of her family members. She was far away from home; far away from Pawan and his daily charade of control, manipulation and oppressive silence. She felt at peace.

She unpacked the sarees she had brought for the meetings and laid out the files on the dresser. She would begin working on them after a shower. This really was a dream project for Sanjay, the firm, and her. She didn't remember having worked so hard on anything in her life before.

After the shower, though, sleep took over. She was woken by the ringing phone.

"I hope you got some rest. You missed lunch."

"Sorry, I fell asleep."

"Why don't we walk down for a snack? Then we can start going over the papers for tomorrow."

"Sure, I will be at the reception in 10 minutes."

They walked to the restaurant down the road. Over bun maska, they discussed the forthcoming meetings. Then they walked back to the hotel, Sanjay with his arm on her shoulder, and she taking in his closeness, which she had missed when he had been away from the office.

Back in the hotel, they picked up the documents from her room. In his room, she began spreading them out on the table. He couldn't help himself from reaching for her face. She came closer and cupped her hands around his face. The intensity of the kiss that followed was something neither of them had ever felt before.

The files were forgotten. Pausing only for breath, they continued kissing passionately. She held him close to her, as close as his hardness would allow. They explored each other's faces, earlobes and back of the neck. Then he kissed her breasts—softly and tenderly, until she felt her nipples harden in his mouth. She moaned. He nested his face between her breasts. Not wanting to let go for even a second, they held each other as they undressed. They continued exploring each other with their lips, mouths, hands. They found themselves in each other and came in a thunderous moment of togetherness. In that moment, it was as if Neena's frigidity and her obsession with the fertility calendar had never existed. And Pawan's aloofness and the emptiness Mahima felt in bed with him was simply a bad dream.

Then they slept, in the hotel room in a busy marketplace near the stock exchange in Bombay. They had come home to each other.

She woke up the next morning to find him sitting by the window, sipping tea. He came over to her side of the bed and kissed her on the forehead. She pulled him into bed with her, and they remained there, softly running their fingers over each other's faces and kissing.

"I will make you some tea," he finally said and got up.

However hard he tried, he hadn't been able to stop himself from falling in love with her. For the first few months, he had ignored the connection he had felt with her, keeping his attraction a secret from her. But yesterday, nothing could have stopped them. Forgetting everything and finding each other, and then, sleeping in each other's arms—spent but not drained—was something he would relive in future many times over.

That morning, he had woken to the buzzing of the alarm of his digital watch, a little before 6 am. Setting the alarm had become a habit, so he wouldn't miss out on checking if Neena had taken her early-morning medicines. From the window, sipping his first cuppa of the morning, he had not admired the skyline of the country's financial capital or reached for the business newspaper. He had simply looked at a sleeping Mahima and relived the moments from the previous night.

He reached for the tea bags while she went into the bathroom to freshen up. She let the water run as she scrubbed her face clean. She didn't have to scrub it much; it was already glowing.

She heard the kettle hiss as the water came to a boil. She imagined Sanjay dipping the tea bag and stirring the sugar with the hands he had run through her hair just a few minutes ago. She joined him for tea, not in the armchairs but in bed.

There was no awkwardness. Just a feeling of calm, of waking up in a hotel room in another city with another woman's husband and feeling as if it had been this way forever.

Her room remained unused during the whole trip. Sanjay and Mahima discovered intimacy in the smallest of things. Having tea in bed, lying entwined with each other, running her hands through the hair on his chest. He would come up behind her as she stood in front of the mirror, and both of them would look at their reflection as they caressed each other. Their lips would lock, and all thoughts of balance sheets, the stock market listing and other such matters would fly out the window.

It was time to return. To the emptiness of their respective marriages—and the pain. Travelling together came as naturally as intimacy in the hotel. The train chugged along, and the symmetrical fields outside alternated with the chaos of traffic and civilisation that crept up whenever a town approached. Passing by different stations, they shared anecdotes from their childhood: of places they had visited and families they had grown up in. They found that comedy movies and cricket were shared interests, too. Over dinner, they discovered that both of them were averse to brinjals—and partial to cauliflower. When he tucked her into the checked-pattern blanket at night, she squeezed his hand before letting it go.

In the morning, he bought her a *kulhar* of steaming hot chai from a railway station on the way. She peered over his shoulder as they read the newspaper together. Then he balanced her handbag on his lap as she reached deep into it to find her small folding mirror. Precious moments they would relive over and over again in the coming months and years. Given the harmony between their words and silences, the chatty lady opposite could be forgiven for assuming they were a freshly wedded couple. They felt that way, in any case.

When the train reached Delhi, they took their respective pieces of luggage. Holding close to their hearts the journey they had started in the hotel room in Bombay, they hailed cabs and went in opposite directions.

15

Falling in love was followed by falling into a routine. It was a new beginning in an old setting. The office and the colleagues were the same. The work was the same. Pawan and Neena were the same. But Sanjay and Mahima were not.

They would come to work, fatigued from the drudgery of their domestic lives. Work, and their closeness, would rejuvenate them. The relationship continued, as did their efforts to keep it discreet and secret.

They carefully crafted a façade of friendship. They would steal snatches of time as they walked through the corridors of Connaught Place, exploring the little surprises on offer. Have coffee at United Coffee House, where Sanjay would wait for her to finish her cold coffee with ice cream before tenderly wiping the dripping mixture from her face. Soaking in the winter sun at Central Park after a busy afternoon would leave them feeling an intimacy that would linger for the rest of the day. They celebrated more momentous occasions at Embassy, Kwality, Host and all the other restaurants. They found a special delight in the shakarkandi ki chaat served by street vendors. They would stand by and wait for the vendor to season the smoked cubes of yam with lemon and spice mixes.

"Sanjay, see how lemon and spices can add zest to something so bland as yam. Isn't life like that, too?

He laughed.

"Yes, my love. And see how the yam is getting cooked on coals. That's also what life is like."

"Always pragmatic, Sanjay! I meant that life can be dull and unliveable if we don't find our spice, our happiness. And once we find it, we must grasp it immediately."

"Yes, just like I have found you and grasped you, and will never let go of you."

Sanjay was grateful to have found Mahima. He had tried hard to make things work with Neena, but in vain. For Mahima, Sanjay's concern and affection laid bare the lack of intimacy, respect and validation in her own marriage. It was but natural that both of them had fallen deeply in love.

They were oblivious to the murmurs and whispers that seemed to disappear into thin air before it reached their ears. The stolen moments at an occasional conference would satisfy them until they found themselves craving each other again. Longing to be touched deep inside, they would carefully plan a business trip, often travelling separately. Their torrid togetherness would restore and replenish them enough to return to the multiple roles they had to play every day—mother, caregiver, provider, dutiful husband, and everything else that others laid out for them.

16

The stock exchange listing and their hard work soon made Roxanne one of the leaders in its field. Sanjay wished Kailash had lived to see the better times that had finally come. The older man's passing had left Sanjay feeling lost. Over the years, Kailash had come to treat Sanjay as his son. After him, things will never be the same again. Sanjay had lost forever one of his most important connections with the firm.

Every time he shared his passion for drug discovery with Mahima, Sanjay's face would come alive. Already a witness to his dedication, she was struck by his passion. She saw in him a dream that he had not been able to snuff out in spite of his—and life's—best efforts. Research and Development (R&D) was a buzzword in the current times.

"Have you ever thought of Roxanne expanding into drug discovery?"

They had finished the lunch she brought for both; the lunch he told Neena he ate in the canteen. The passion with which they loved each other hadn't waned in the last two years. The rush they felt when they brushed against each other at work, the stolen kisses just before she left his cubicle, the clasped hands in the coffee shop—everything made them feel as heady as on that first occasion in Bombay. It was a love, and a passion, that had stayed strong in spite of everything.

"Mahima, drug R&D needs an entirely different setup and approach. That has never been the agenda of our firm. Besides, doing R&D would mean I wouldn't be able to spare time or energy for the management work that keeps me so busy today."

"Hmm, I know. But the firm is stable enough. You could delegate the other work and concentrate on R&D."

That evening, sipping tea at home, Sanjay flipped through a recent pharmacology journal.

"Sanjay. Use a coaster. And tea is best had on the dining table, not on the sofa! I don't want a stain on the white sofa."

He looked up, smiled at Neena and said, "Sorry! I've almost finished. By the way, I love how you have done up the living room."

He knew Neena had been trying to occupy herself with redoing their home and was appreciative of her efforts. Her new medicines were working better, too, and the intervals of normalcy were becoming longer and more consistent. He hoped this phase would last a while.

Later, at night, Neena said, "I don't see why you keep reading those journals."

"Maybe the company could diversify into drug discovery. Roxanne is doing well now," Sanjay replied.

Subdued and withdrawn over lunch the next day, he told Mahima how this conversation had set off an attack of hysteria in Neena. She had accused him—again—of abandoning Roxanne's founding vision. Ironically, little did Neena know that this was just what he had wanted to immediately after their wedding, but had not. Only for her sake.

Mahima had met Neena only occasionally. One of these occasions had been the recent Family Day celebrations at Roxanne, when they had unveiled a bust of Kamal Pandit, the founder of the company. Demure and soft-spoken, Neena had linked her arm through Sanjay's all evening. It was a reminder of how each moment of his life, other than the ones he spent at work, seemed to be inexorably linked with her. Mahima had not expected to resent Neena, but she had found herself doing exactly that. Was it a resentment at having to share Sanjay with Neena? Or was it about having to share a part of herself with Pawan? Or, did she resent the fact that the love Sanjay and she shared would never have social sanction?

But the resentment had been transient. Sanjay and she knew, and accepted, the limitations of their relationship; they never pretended to think otherwise.

Mahima had greeted Neena with the warmth and grace that the daughter of the company's founder deserved and had continued overseeing the arrangements for the evening. The Family Day was an occasion she cherished. Seeing Sanjay and Neena unveil the bust and pose for photographs had reminded her of the first Family Day celebrations she had attended at Roxanne. It had truly been a time to celebrate. She remembered how Pawan had tried to scuttle her plan to attend the function by feigning a headache and demanding a specific medicine. She had rushed to get it for him. Piyu had gone off to sleep exhausted, after waiting for them to stop arguing. When Mahima had insisted on attending the event at any cost, Pawan had finally relented. But he had taken a long detour to the venue, ostensibly to get his watch fixed on the way. And, like all their social outings, that evening too had been an unsavoury experience, with Pawan losing his temper over some small forgettable matter or the other.

17

While Roxanne was attaining new heights, Mahima's ambitions were also rising sky-high. She believed that productivity would increase if the employees felt more involved with the company.

"Are you serious? You mean this?"

They had been strolling through Palika Bazar. They frequented the many shops there to add to their collection of Hindi movie songs. Sanjay would always watch patiently as she carefully selected the albums, and then pick up an identical set for himself.

She had suggested that Roxanne consider issuing Employee Stock Options (ESOs).

The look on her face meant she was dead serious. "Mahima, do you think this will work in a homegrown company like ours?"

"Exactly why it will work. You always say that it is a family. This will make that ethos stronger."

"Can I ever reject an idea that comes from you? Especially one that makes your eyes light up like this?"

"Very funny. I am sure you know better than that!" she said, laughing.

∞

It had been a long time since she had seen him excited about anything. And that bothered her. He hardly ever spoke of his student days now and had even missed out on his college reunion. Earlier, he would animatedly describe how drugs were developed. He would talk passionately about drugs, molecules and the potential of these new medicines to help millions of suffering patients. But now, he hardly ever spoke about all that.

Mahima realised that the embers were still there, but were waiting to be rekindled. Just as the embers in her had been kindled when life had given a clean slate—her job at Roxanne. She wanted him to be the Sanjay he *could* be, not the one he had been forced to become. But, at the same time, she understood how the difficult situation at home was holding him back. It wasn't much different for her. After all, in spite of her accolades and achievements, Pawan remained unsupportive and hostile.

In fact, since the time his business had taken off, he had become even more critical of her, and demanding, whenever he was home.

"You should come home in time for Piyu's homework," he said one day.

"I thought you said *you* will help her with science," she replied indignantly. It had been Pawan's idea that he would spend time with Piyu and help her with her homework. But, after making that offer, he had been away for more than a week.

"You are neglecting her for your own ambitions. You hardly spend any time at home," he told her another day.

She was glad she had not told him that she had been held up because of the driving lessons she was taking. Later, when she would raise the matter of buying a second-hand car, she would lie to him that her father had taught her to drive a car many years ago. It was another of her small lies that ensured that the days passed without confrontation. The lies were small, but she was tiring of them. They were reminders that Pawan found it difficult to accept a reality in which she was not what *he* wanted her to be.

She remembered how she had felt terribly guilty for the first few months after she returned from that first trip to Bombay. She had felt she was letting Pawan down by following her heart and allowing her relationship with Sanjay to bloom. Of course, Pawan had many shortcomings which could never be condoned, but the two of them were still bound by marriage, weren't they? But, was a marriage without respect and understanding a marriage at all? It had taken her a long time to tell herself that she was doing the right thing.

Love had prevailed. Her feelings for Sanjay were undeniable. The emotional distance between Pawan and her, and his disinterest in her as a person, had always made it easy to keep secrets from him. In fact, her secrets and lies were what made life tolerable for her.

18

Sanjay pushed the pamphlet towards her. It was a brochure of a respected educational institute.

"This is interesting. It is a course with a Company Secretary degree."

"Hmm."

"You should do it."

She held his hand.

"You know Pawan will never allow it. As it is, he isn't happy with the time I spend away from the house."

"But it is mostly by correspondence. You need to only attend a few classes in person."

She was silent.

"It will be good for you. And for the company."

Roxanne had begun manufacturing generic drugs to supply to international markets. Patent laws were changing and becoming business-friendly. The Company Secretary course would be a step into the future for Mahima. And Sanjay was sure that Roxanne's future and her future were inextricably linked.

"You know you want to, my dear."

"And you know I can't, love."

Pawan was busier than ever with work. The demands on her time had only increased. Keeping up with Piyu, who was growing up fast, was another challenge. The more involved Mahima became in her work, the less involved Pawan wanted to be at home or with their daughter. It was Reshma who held the threads of their lives, managing everything unobtrusively yet perfectly.

But that night, after Piyu had slept, she pulled out the brochure. It *was* a correspondence course, like Sanjay had said, with just a fortnight of contact classes spread out over two years. Her jaw stiffened ever so slightly. She would find time to study at night. Roxanne had many more milestones to achieve, and she would do her part in making that happen.

∞

The two-year course was intensive. But it gave her a lot of confidence and exposure to the workings of the corporate world. She looked forward to the convocation in Madras. She was excited about going on stage after many years to collect a degree.

"It is Shyam's wedding in Jodhpur," Pawan told her when she told him about her impending trip for the convocation. Shyam was Pawan's cousin.

"Who? I don't remember meeting him," she replied.

"That doesn't matter. It is protocol. I need to attend. And Piyu should also get to know the family."

"But I will be receiving my degree!"

"What will people say? Having to study at this age!"

She travelled to Chennai, which she preferred to call Madras. Sanjay came too and checked into a different hotel.

"You should have taken rest. I had been so worried about you," she told him.

"I couldn't let you attend it alone. Besides, I am fine now. I was missing you, dear."

Sanjay had been driving to the golf course in Gurgaon some time back, when he had swerved to avoid a collision. He had been able to avoid it, but his car had crashed into the kerb. The accident had left a scar on his face and a rod implanted in a bone in his left arm.

Mahima had visited him in the hospital. Neena had been there in his room. Mahima's anguish at not being able to embrace Sanjay had been as intense as the pain of his injury. His gaze had met hers, locked in an instant and given them strength—as their relationship always had. It had taken him a few weeks to recover and return to work. After which, he decided he couldn't stay away from her anymore.

As they sat in her room in Madras, Mahima lightly traced the scar on his face with her fingertips. He rested his head on her chest and told her of the argument Neena had had with him just before the accident. He had known that she desperately wanted to adopt a child. But, seeing her instability, and how much care she herself needed, he couldn't agree to adopting one. Midway through the argument, he had stormed out of the house. Her screaming at him, demanding that they adopt a baby, had been reverberating in his mind as he had swerved to avoid the oncoming two-wheeler and hit the kerb.

Mahima felt her eyes welling up. She hugged him close and placed her fingers on his lips.

"Sshh. Enough." She held him close.

19

Eight years had passed since they had first travelled to Bombay together. Almost nine since they had sat in the office under the flickering light bulb and kissed for the first time. The duality of their lives should have been exhausting. But it wasn't. The relationship, like the firm, flourished.

Being with each other came naturally to them.

On their secret trips, she would wake up in a hotel room in a new place, pull open the curtains and watch the rays of the morning sun dapple on his face, as if she did it every day. And, he would wait for her to finish her morning meditation before making her tea, as if it had always been this way.

At the office, during mundane discussions and tedious meetings, their eyes would meet and each would know exactly what the other was thinking. She would reach for the pen in his shirt pocket and loosen his tie suggestively before returning to her desk. He would playfully finger the palla of her saree before opening the door of his cubicle.

For Mahima, the days when Pawan was in Delhi held more loneliness than the weeks when he was away. It was sobering to realise that she preferred his absence to his presence. Perhaps he did too, because he was gone more often, and for longer.

Neena had reconciled herself to Sanjay's refusal to adopt a baby by becoming more aloof and spending all her time in her studio. She seemed to have inherited a talent for art from her mother and was devoting her time to its pursuit.

Meanwhile, Roxanne continued to grow. It exceeded Kamal Pandit's expectations—*everyone's* expectations, actually. Sanjay knew that without Mahima, they wouldn't have been able to achieve this growth trajectory. It was almost a decade since Roxanne's and his futures had merged, and Sanjay should have been looking forward to a phase of future growth. But there was something missing. The managerial role he had moulded himself for reluctantly, and excelled at, was no longer stimulating or challenging enough. While Mahima would talk about Roxanne's prospects, he would follow global developments in drug research.

The embers still burned inside him. Mahima was sure of that.

20

"Sanjay, at least meet them. And take it from there. These things don't happen in a day, anyway."

She had met some venture capitalists at her meetings at the Confederation of Indian Industries. They were looking to set up research centres affiliated with private universities. Someone with a passion and degree in pharmacology would fit the bill, they said. Exposure to the industry would help even more. Mahima thought Sanjay was perfect for the opportunity. And the opportunity was perfect for him. He could do what he had always been passionate about.

"Okay, Mahima, but you know it's not going to work out."

"Things at home have changed somewhat, haven't they, Sanjay?"

"Yes..."

They had. Neena was quieter now. There were fewer confrontations, though the calm was often an uneasy one. Yet, he could feel the pattern of Neena's disease changing, with fewer disruptive phases.

"Sanjay, I don't want you to regret not doing this all your life. At least, give it a shot," pressed Mahima.

He mulled it over. *She's right about the spark still being there, but I can't pretend that it hasn't dimmed,* he thought. Circumstances and age had taken a toll; he was wise enough now to realise that all dreams didn't have to come true. And that, those that did, often came at a price.

∞

One evening, Neena and Sanjay were returning from meeting her doctor. She was responding well to her new medication. He was surprised when she reached out for his hand. "Sanjay, something has been on my mind for a few days. I want to ask you for something. I would really like to move back to the old house, where I grew up. That is, if you are okay with it."

"Neena, if living there makes you happy, we can do it."
"Yes, I think I *will* be happy there."

"Neena, there is a great opportunity in drug research. I could start an innovation centre."

He bit his lip as soon as he had spoken. He hadn't meant it as a trade-off, and hoped she didn't see it that way, either. It was just that moments like this had become rare, and the words had slipped out.

He was tense.

Her reaction—or the lack of it—was unexpected. There was no bout of hysteria. No screaming.

Maybe she didn't care. Or didn't care enough. Or maybe, she was finally at peace with herself, enough to allow him to follow his heart.

He waited silently.

"Sanjay, can you stop the car?"

Damn, he didn't need her to create a scene here, on the road. He stopped off the main road and waited.

She shifted in her seat and moved closer to him. "Will this make you happy?"

He didn't reply. He had stopped searching for happiness and answers many years ago. He looked at her. Her face had not lost any of its beauty. It was ironic that the frailness that came with being frequently ill made her look even more serene.

"Yes. But it also means leaving Roxanne."

"Research is something you have always wanted to do. But couldn't. There was too much in the way."

Her insight and understanding of the situation were surprising, but just a little. By nature, she was a person with empathy; deeply sensitive and thoughtful.

He remained silent.

"Yes, Sanjay, maybe you should do this. If this is what you want."

"Are you sure?"

"Yes, it will be like it was in the beginning. Just you and me."

He knew she was trying to create an illusion that would make life easier for herself. You couldn't turn back the clock by returning to old homes or reversing decisions made years ago. He knew that she knew it, too.

He turned his attention to the wheel again.

21

Neena had laid down only one condition. The name of the firm would not be changed—now, or at any time in the future. Sanjay and Mahima didn't have any problems with that. Sanjay stepped down as managing director of the firm. He transferred many of his shares to the trust that managed the affairs of Roxanne. Mahima owned a significant proportion of shares already. The board would elect her as the next managing director.

"Are you sure? You could continue to be on the board and be involved in the firm," Mahima told him.

"No, Mahima, this is the way it should be. Dreams don't come true if we hang on to the past. We must have the courage to break free if we want to achieve something."

"I want you to consider it again."

"Even if I think it over a hundred times, the truth is that you have been the force behind the firm in recent times. It is *you* who should lead from the front now."

They busied themselves with the transition. This step would change their lives irrevocably. But Roxanne, of course, was still close to his heart; it would always be.

"Mahima, I hope I am taking the correct decision."

"I know you are, darling. This is what you have always desired. You know you have the potential to make it big in R&D."

"But I was younger then."

"You don't seem particularly old now." She nibbled on his ear lobe.

"*You* make me feel young and ambitious and alive."

"And you make me feel like myself, Sanjay. Always have."

"Mahima, I love you. And will always love you."

"Hmm, I love you, too. And will miss you."

"Can you miss someone who is a part of you?"

"No. You are right. But I will miss coming to work to you, and our everyday togetherness."

"I will, too. But we will meet outside. That will never change."

"We will, Sanjay. Sometimes. But you also know it won't be the same."

"It doesn't *have* to be the same."

"That's true. And, with a relationship like ours, we always knew that, didn't we?"

"Mahima, I never imagined I would find a love as strong as ours. It must have been destined for us."

"Yes, Sanjay. I always wonder how something that was unimaginable can feel so natural!"

"Relationships may change, Mahima, but love will remain. Even if we cannot be a part of each other's daily lives, we will always be a part of each other's souls."

"Yes."

They stayed in touch, never away from important developments in each other's lives. Roxanne's listing on the New York Stock Exchange, the diagnosis of Mahima's fibromyalgia after many months of illness and a battery of tests, Sanjay's increasing responsibilities at his innovation centre...through all this, they remained a comforting presence and sounding board for each other.

They met, of course, on a few occasions after Sanjay left the firm. Both of them would travel, ostensibly for business conventions. Sometimes, they would travel to different places and then, one of them would take a detour to meet the other. The passion with which they embraced each other made them forget the time that had passed since they had last met. Their hunger for each other would take over, and then they would lie in each other's arms for hours. They would caress each other's faces, committing the lines, wrinkles and smiles to memory.

Just that, of late, with their hectic routines, it had become difficult to catch up often. Earlier, they would meet once in a few days. But now, they had to stay apart for weeks or, sometimes, even for months. The last time they had met was for lunch at the golf club, almost a year ago. It was mostly over the phone that they kept in touch now. But they felt as strongly connected to each other as they had felt when they used to walk into the Roxanne's small office all those years ago, looking forward to spending the day together.

22

Present Day

Mahima continued reading the news report.

The new drug, called Ty-54R, is a landmark development for the treatment of cancers that have spread to different parts of the body. The prototype has been developed indigenously and has now been cleared for use. Speaking to this correspondent, Sanjay Shukla, Founder of Sanjeevani Centre for Innovation, said, "It has been my company's mission to develop and discover drugs starting from the active molecule—right here, in India. This not only reduces the costs and makes treatments more accessible for the underprivileged patients of our country but also demonstrates to the world what our brilliant researchers are capable of."

She looked at the picture again. The furrowed forehead hadn't changed since the day she had first met him. His tenacity had been behind Roxanne's success. And his career with Sanjeevani, his drug research and development company, had been equally eventful and successful. It had been a long road that Sanjay and Mahima had travelled on; together and separately.

Once, a few years ago, Piyu had told Mahima, "Both of you were in love. Didn't you want to spend your life together?" Very close to her mother, Piyu had been privy to her mother's sorrows, loneliness, joys, and struggles. She had grown into a strong willed, young woman and was glad that her mother had not had to walk her journey alone.

It wasn't an unreasonable question. Having found love, wouldn't they want to get married to each other, too?

"It was complicated, Piyu."

"Unhappy marriages don't have to be endured. And both of you had served your time, hadn't you?"

Had they told themselves the complete truth when they had agreed that they could be together in love but not in daily life? It had been beyond complicated. As always, the surface and the depth would reveal different reasons. Guilt, the affection for their respective spouses that hadn't died down completely, the feeling of duty towards their respective spouses, even the *convenience* of the arrangement—they hadn't been able to deny any of these. And there was also the pain of failed relationships. A pain that had made them very vulnerable to getting hurt again. Did they not want a future together, or did they want it so much that they couldn't risk damaging the fragile threads of happiness that they had woven into their troubled lives? Maybe they had cherished each moment of togetherness too much to risk damaging it? Or maybe, they were too weary of life to trust in it? There was some truth in all of these aspects. But, for them, the absolute truth was their love. Their feelings were undeniable and unstoppable, and they had been savouring each moment of togetherness, as if to make up for time lost—and time that may never come again.

Mahima continued to read.

Mr. Sanjay Shukla, who is a recipient of the lifetime achievement award of the Indian Pharmaceutical Research Association, announced a dedicated centre for research on mental health.

Another thing she had known he wanted to do, even though he had never spoken about it.

Although there was much that they had not explicitly spoken about over the last few years, she did have a window to his life. She knew that his life with Neena was now much better; different from the life, and space, that she had shared with Pawan before he had finally stopped coming home abruptly, without any explanation. On his last visit home, he had told Piyu he was setting up a packaging unit in Jodhpur. A few weeks later, Reshma, perceptive as ever, had told Neena, "*Woh laut ke nahin aayega.*" (He won't return home).

Similar pain (though in different circumstances) and years spent under the same roof had forged a close bond between Mahima and Reshma. It was Reshma who had had an early insight into a man who would never be able to accept a woman forging her own identity. That insight had come late to Mahima.

The first thing Piyu had done when she received her degree as a lawyer had been to draw up the divorce papers. Pawan's apathy had not been surprising for Mahima, but Piyu had been upset when he had not even responded to the notice she had sent him. She had travelled to Jodhpur and arranged for the divorce decree, a document that held as little significance in Mahima's life as Pawan did now.

As for Sanjay, Mahima always hoped that he felt content and fulfilled at home, just as she did when she returned home to Reshma's dinner and Piyu's phone calls. She was sure that their love still gave him strength, like it did for her. When the fibromyalgia flares would wake her up sweaty and uncomfortable in the dead of the night, she would imagine Sanjay's hand on her forehead before reaching for the medicines on the dresser. Sanjay too would often find himself missing the way she ran her hands through his hair when he would be lost deep in thought.

Mahima knew that the years that Sanjay and she had spent together, and the love they had found, had given Sanjay the strength to partially mend his marriage. But, in spite of her best efforts with Pawan, she had been left staring into a void of indifference. She had used the strength of Sanjay's love to numb the pain and move on to create a different life for herself. One where her family, that comprised Reshma and Piyu, was the centre of her life.

She knew that Sanjay and Neena's routines were made up of each other. Of shared meals, time, and events. Of silences that may not be filled with connection or meaning, but were not uneasy or tense, either. Of words that might not complete each other's sentences, but that didn't scorch their souls, either. She knew that his evenings were a homecoming for him. His was a life that may be imperfect, but one that he had made his peace with, and found peace in.

She played the video for the evening's presentation on the LED TV in her room. It was a beautifully edited collection of quotes from many of the employees. They would play it before she dedicated the merger deal to all the employees of the firm. She pressed *Send*, approving the video, so that the team could get on with the celebrations.

Today was officially a half working day, and everyone would go back home soon to get ready for the occasion.

I must get going, too, she thought.

She looked at the newspaper again and felt warm with happiness at Sanjay's achievement. Then, she placed it in the top drawer of her desk. Sanjay's desk, come to think of it. She reached for the phone, but decided against sending him a message.

"Congratulations!"

Her voice memo was answered almost immediately by his text message.

"Thanks, love."

"I knew Sanjeevani would achieve great heights."

"Yes, you did. Even when *I* didn't."

"It's Family Day today."

"Congratulations on the merger. Perfect timing!"

She smiled and sent him a heart emoji.

23

She requested the driver to drive through the inner circle of Connaught Place before heading home. So many of the stores and restaurants here held a special place in her heart. Walking down the corridors to Oxford Bookstore to buy books for Piyu, binging on pastries at Wenger's, the weekly lunch at one of the many restaurants, and the milkshake at Keventers. Buying audio cassettes at Palika Bazaar. Waiting for their turn at the South Indian restaurant on Janpath. Moments stolen away from office. She had almost never visited any of those places after Sanjay left, but still, it all felt like yesterday.

"Stop the car at the next block."

"Madam, no space there. Further down, there is space, but you will have to walk back."

"That's ok."

She walked across the stores. A few of the old ones had been replaced by branded outlets and food chains, but many of the regular haunts for shopping and food remained as before. Small entrances leading to stairs had popped up; a gateway into new restaurants on the first and second floors of the buildings, something she had never imagined possible. The college students ambling along, enjoying one another's company, did not seem misfits amidst the focused brisk walk of the office-goers. The chatter of the shoppers filled the corridors, as did the voices of the vendors who had laid out their wares at the corners. When the aroma of freshly baked confectionery mingled with that of cold coffee and greeted her at Wenger's, she felt as if nothing had changed for ages. As she walked in, she knew exactly what she would order.

"Two paneer cutlets and two butterscotch pastries."

"Yes, ma'am."

It was only when she checked the bill out of habit that she realised she had ordered for two people. She was amused. This was their standard order. Sanjay's and hers. Today, she relished it in the company of his memories.

24

She had already decided what she would wear that evening. Reshma had arranged the ikat saree and its contrasting blouse on the bed. She draped it neatly and fastened the chunky silver choker around her neck. She had cropped her hair short when it had begun greying. She had wanted to keep her grey look but had finally accepted Piyu's suggestion of experimenting a little with hair colour. She combed the red streak into place and leaned closer to the mirror to apply kajal. The uniform, smooth black line of liquid kajal, which she still preferred to the chalky pencil versions, framed her almond-shaped eyes perfectly. Then she stepped back to see if she was ready to step out.

Her reflection in the mirror made her smile.

In it she saw a woman who had been touched by love and been saved and strengthened by the power it had kindled. A woman who had been fortunate to have loved and been loved back; to have lived life on her own terms, without regrets or misgivings.

It was then that she saw Sanjay standing behind her. His love for her was unmistakable in his eyes. He held her by the shoulders and kissed her on the nape of her neck, moving her wispy hair while doing so. She shut her eyes to freeze the image a little longer. And then opened them again. The strength of their love was so strong that she could visualise him in her mind's eye anytime. After all, they were a part of each other's souls. Such was the power of the love they felt and manifested every single moment.

∞

Acknowledgments

Main akela hi chala tha jaanib-e-manzil magar...Log saath aate gaye aur karwan banta gaya.

—Majrooh Sultanpuri

This book started as a short story and an abstract idea. To see it in its current form is both heart-warming and humbling. It is a reminder of how our words and actions have the power to touch, transform and redeem. There have been so many people who have encouraged me, believed in me, and read my work. It is not possible to thank each of these, but they are all deeply cherished.

And then, there are those, who are inextricably linked with the journey of this book and mine; and for whom the word 'acknowledgement' may fall short.

My parents, for giving me the courage and conviction to write my stories-and not just the ones in this book.

My children—my champions and cheerleaders—from whom I have learnt more than I might have taught them. You are everything and more.

My husband, and my brother, the constants in a world peppered with uncertainties.

Rituparna and Urvashi, for being so generous and prompt with feedback and advice.

Ramanjaneya and Arva, for being the most supportive writing companions.

Ganesh, for nurturing the book since its inception, caring for it and enriching it.

Dipankar, for believing in the book, and making it happen.

Kasturi, Salini, and Namrata, for always being there.

Women's Web—where I first gathered the courage to put my writing out into the world—for gifting me most uplifting sisterhood ever.

The First Draft Club of the Himalayan Writing Retreat, where I found my writing routine, and so many invaluable nuggets of information.

And, finally, those select, *very* special friends of mine—the stars in *my* sky—always there, shining for me, lighting the path ahead when the darkness seems never ending. You know who you are, and my gratitude to you is beyond this book. It is for life itself.

SHALINI MULLICK
Gurugram 2022

About the Author

Shalini is a writer with a diverse portfolio spanning fiction, non-fiction, and poetry. Her flash fictions, drabbles, and stories have been featured on many online platforms.

She was selected as *Juggernaut Selects* author for her e-single *Happily Divorced*. She was also one of the winners of the *eShe* short story contest. She has published two short stories each in the anthologies *Sharing Lipstick* and *Women. Mutiny*. One of her short stories was selected for publication in the anthology *Everything Changed After That*, which was unveiled at the *Ananke Women in Literature Festival* in 2021. Her work on many reputed platforms like *eShe Magazine, Women's Web, Eyra* magazine and *Incredible Women of India* has been well received.

She was awarded the *Orange Flower Award for Short Fiction* in 2022, and for writing on LGBTQ+ issues in 2021. She was also a finalist for the same award for writing on humour in 2021. She was also the winner of the *#tellastoryinsixwords* Challenge by Crossword Bookstores and a judge for myWish4U talent contest organised by Smile Foundation. She has won the 'Muse of The Month' contest organised by *Women's Web* on multiple occasions. Shalini empathises with the challenges and unique situations that women are often confronted with and weaves this understanding in her writing.

In her other avatar, she is a practicing doctor, specialising in respiratory pathology with many scientific research papers and textbook chapters to her credit. Medical Humanities is an area in which she has a keen interest, and her poetry has been published in reputed journals. She is a copyeditor and on the Review board of the journal *Research and Humanities in Medical Education*.

A late entrant to the world of writing, Shalini finds it takes her away from noise, and towards silence. It is also a good excuse to avoid hitting the gym; and stops her from helicopter parenting her teenage children. She is happiest in the company of books, chocolates, and old Hindi movie songs. Though she has beautiful memories of her years in Bangalore and has now put down roots in Gurgaon, she remains a Dilliwali at heart.

Stars from the Borderless Sea is her first book. You can read more about her at www.shalinimullick.com

Readomania

Readomania exists to nurture, curate, and bring to you content you love. We are a publishing house that takes pride in encouraging talent, new or old, and provide a wonderful platform for awesome stories.

We make this possible in multiple ways.

First, as an independent publishing house. Readomania boasts of multiple imprints across various categories—fiction, nonfiction, children, to name a few. An eclectic mix of content for its readers, when you read a Readomania title, you enter a world that's yours, supported by unique and quality narratives.

Second, as an online publishing platform for writers—a place to share stories, poems, opinions, travelogues, a way to explore your creative talent. Available as premium, as well as free-to-read content across multiple genres, the reader is spoilt for choice.

Join us in this journey, as we explore, develop, and present stories to our readers and audiences. Welcome to the world of Readomania, get ready to craft stories that enrich lives.

You can visit us at: www.readomania.com